Paperback edition manufactured in the United States of America

ISBN: 9798627318042

Dedicated to the memory of my mother

Iva Mary McConnell Sanderson

A *tour de force* in her world

SHILLINGSTONE

COUNTY OF DORSET

ENGLAND

It was a cold winter morning at the dawn of a new century in 1800 and many of the seventy-six villagers in the small hamlet of Shillingstone were stoking fires to keep their cottages warm, with scant attention to any significance of the day. It was a village of modest means with farm laborers and craftsmen doing the same work their predecessors had done for generations, to provide a living in good times and bad. Few traveled no more than a person could walk and return home in a day. Little had changed.

Years later on a warm August morning in1863, change came to Shillingstone with neither a whimper nor a bang. It came with the ringing of a brass bell and the whistle of a steam engine. Rutted roads gave way to an iron horse clicking along on steel rails. When the Dorset Central Railway arrived, a gate opened to a world far beyond their village. A person could take a trip to Bournemouth by the sea or to London and view Buckingham Palace. The rail station became the central hub of commerce and social life for the inhabitants of Shillingstone.

We are able to view the village through the lives of two young people, Sarah, 18, and Byron, 19, as well as those who surround them. Early on they discover the joy of young love, conflict, rejection, sickness, and death. Life in this small hamlet is revealed as they chart their passage through the second half century in Queen Victoria's England.

Keith McConnell

CHAPTERS

NO WAY OUT

At the end of an exhausting day young Sarah Glanville looked through a dirty old window which gave a distorted view of the setting sun. Like her warped view, she felt her life and future were hopeless. In her sadness a tear slowly slid down her cheek as dancing shadows from the fireplace added to her angst. Light from a flickering candle gave little consolation. When a blanket of darkness covered her little cottage she felt trapped with no way out. In desperation she cried, "Please...God help me, how can I get out of here?" No one heard her cry.

The next morning Sarah awoke tired and confused. Still in bed with a blanket pulled over her head she was hardly aware that the darkness had dissipated as the light of morning filled her cottage. Sleep had not removed the burden of her sick mother, her infirm young brother and an absent father. As Sarah lay in bed she thought about the burden of her family responsibilities and how it contrasted with the carefree memories of her childhood. "How did this happen?"

Sarah had been a happy child. She loved her father, Edward, who frequently placed Sarah on his knee, with his arm around her waist, and read her delightful stories. At the end of every story he told her that she was the most important little girl in the world. He thanked God for the gift of a daughter. He said, "Every father should have a daughter just like you." Sarah absorbed his praise like a sponge.

From birth Sarah was the center of her mother's life. Mildred treated her little darling like a living doll. At age five she displayed a bubbly personality as she hopped and skipped everywhere she went. It was impossible to visit the baker, grocer or post office without some mother telling Mildred, "What a sweet child."

About this age it became obvious to Mildred that Sarah was fascinated watching her spin wool on her spinning wheel. But it had started much earlier. Mildred's mother promised Mildred that when she married she would inherit the family's baby cradle and spinning wheel. Both had been in the family for three generations and were passed down to succeeding generations. Now they were Mildred's.

When Sarah was born, she was wrapped warmly in a blanket and lay in the cradle, which enabled her mother to have her close by as she spun wool to make clothing or skeins to sell. Sarah would lie in the cradle beside her mother, awake or asleep, and hear the pedal squeak and the whirring sound of the spinning wheel. Later, as a toddler, Mildred would place Sarah on her knee with her arm wrapped around her, feeding carded wool on bobbins and spinning finished skeins of wool. These early years created a deep loving bond between mother and daughter.

As time passed, little Sarah was not satisfied watching her mother, she wanted to try it herself. Looking up at her mother she asked, "Can I put my foot on the pedal?"

"Yes… you can. Put your foot on the pedal next to mine."

"Like that?" Sarah replied.

"Yes, just like that. Over time I am going to teach you how to take lamb's wool and spin it into beautiful wool skeins."

She was a quick learner and over the next three to four years Sarah became a skilled spinner. Working together on the spinning wheel deepened the close loving relationship between them.

By age ten she was an attractive young girl with a pale rose complexion, long sandy colored hair and a petite figure that gave her an aura of confidence. She was cute with blue eyes and a remarkable dimple on each cheek, and a smile that could melt the heart of any crusty curmudgeon. Mildred was proud when neighbors told her Sarah was a bright and beautiful young child. No one didn't love her. Sarah was a carefree young girl who loved everything about her life.

Some young girls go through an awkward phase on the path to maturity. Fortunately Sarah slid through this stage and emerged as a flower of beauty, grace and poise. No longer a child, she became aware of a world beyond herself. With her girlfriends she talked about everything attendant to their age. Like them, Sarah was interested in knowing all about babies. Where did they come from?

Annie, the giggler of the group, shyly whispered, "When I asked my mother, she told me if she swallowed a seed then a baby boy or girl would be born."

Assertive Constance said her mother told her she was delivered by a stork.

A different answer came from Phoebe's mother who divulged, "An angel brought a baby to the front door in the middle of the night."

Sarah was confident she knew the real answer. She had overheard an older girl say she knew how babies were made. In unison they squealed with excitement and said, "Let's make one, let's make one!" Sarah didn't know anything beyond what she heard, but maybe she could figure it out.

She began, "Let's take some flour, add some yeast like my mother does, and include honey for a girl or salt for a boy."

They jumped up and down with excitement and cried, "A girl, a girl!" After collecting some flour, they weren't sure what came next. With more thought and discussion they agreed it was too much work.

Sarah loved her doll made by her grandmother, even though it was falling apart. However playing with dolls was for little girls, not young ladies. Instead Sarah and her three girlfriends decided to each make a doll and give it to a little girl who didn't have one. After gathering straw, cotton, thread and the smallest buttons they could find, the project began. They agreed to meet every Sunday after church and work on their dolls. After four or five Sundays they were finished. Who had made the best doll? It was agreed each one of them had the best doll, in fact so good, each decided to keep theirs.

At twelve, having a pretty dress was important. Most dresses were hand-me-downs previously made by their mothers. Like other girls her age Sarah had a Sunday dress. She loved her Sunday dress and bonnet as they had been purchased at a dress shop in Blandford Forum. Her mother had selected a full-length dress of Indian cotton with short puffed sleeves and a high waist with a beautiful bow around the back. Her mother also made an everyday cotton dress which Sarah wore with a smock to keep it clean and last longer.

Daily chores awaited growing young girls and Sarah was no exception. She was assigned to carry in water and wood for the fireplace, to sweep the stone floor and learn to cook. Other girlfriends had siblings who shared their work. She often wished she had a younger sister or brother. It was a wish she would come to regret

MY DADDY LOVES ME

Edward Glanville's curiosity was obvious at an early age as he constantly asked questions. He asked his father, "Why is the sky blue? Why do leaves fall from trees? Why does it snow?" The questions never stopped and at times they were annoying. When Edward was twelve he saw an old man walking around Shillingstone pulling an unusual looking chain behind him. Periodically he laid the chain on the ground, stopped and wrote something in a small book. What was he doing? Why would an old man walk around the village pulling a funny looking chain behind him? When Edward got home he asked his father about the old man and what he saw. His father smiled and told Edward that everyone called the man Mr. Surveyor. He explained the job of a surveyor and that the chain was to measure distances. Edward was intrigued. He didn't realize it would change his life.

Edward was anxious to find the old man, and several days later he saw him as he pulled the chain behind him. Cautiously Edward approached and asked, "Excuse me, sir, are you Mr. Surveyor?"

Slightly stooped, with a wrinkled leathery face, the old man stopped, turned to Edward and quietly answered, "Yes." After a pause he continued, "Why do you ask?" Edward explained he was curious about the man's work and why everyone called him Mr. Surveyor. Eying Edward carefully, he asked, "Young man, what's your name and how old are you?"

Surprised by the question, Edward mumbled, "My name is Edward Glanville and I'm twelve."

"Well young man, I'm almost seventy and have been called Mr. Surveyor for so many years I don't rightly remember my given name." Assuming Edward had some interest in what he was doing, he explained the importance of surveying, as property owners had to know the boundaries of their land.

Over the next several months Edward followed Mr. Surveyor like a shadow. He learned the purpose of a 60-foot chain, compass, tripod, telescope, plumb bob and other surveying equipment. Edward wanted to learn this profession and asked Mr. Surveyor for his help. Up to now the old man had thought little about who might replace him. Now he had a possible answer. He said, "Son, when you turn sixteen I would be willing to accept you as an apprentice surveyor." Edward was elated at the prospect, but disappointed he had to wait two years. In the meantime, Mr. Surveyor allowed Edward to continue to follow him everywhere he went.

As Edward was approaching sixteen, his mentor outlined a path for him to follow to become a surveyor. Edward soaked up everything like a blotter. After three years of internship, and five years as a journeyman, he was now twenty four, and as a qualified surveyor he was accepted by the prestigious engineering firm of Rutherford and Benson.

On joining the firm, he made a commitment to himself to be the best surveyor in the company. Work consumed most of Edward's time and energy for the next several years. While surveying a farm outside of Shillingstone, a partner with whom he was working introduced him to a twenty-three-year old spinster by the name of Mildred Harrison. There was an immediate mutual attraction and within a year Edward and Mildred were married in the Church of the Holy Rood.

Now twenty-five years old, Edward was well established and an important member of the company. Rutherford and Benson had received a contract to work in Dorset to complete surveying for a new Tithe Act. In 1836 the British Parliament established a tithe law called the Tithe Commutations Act, which required every inch of England and Wales to be surveyed and every land owner identified. For centuries, a tithe was based on the earth's abundance and given to the Church Rector to be stored in a tithe barn and over time to be sold for the benefit of the Church of England. After 1836, tithes were to be collected in pecuniary funds, no longer harvested from the land. It was a gargantuan task. A large section of Dorset was assigned to the firm of Rutherford and Benson and Edward would not be short of work.

After two years of marriage Mildred informed Edward that she was with child. In the summer of 1837 a baby girl was born to the Glanville's and was named Sarah Ann after both their grandmothers. She was a beautiful baby, cherished and loved by both her parents.

Edward travelled over Dorset working in all seasons of the year, and it showed. He was not a big man, but stocky and barrel-chested with a ruddy outdoor complexion. His arms were muscular and legs like tree trunks developed as he traversed every imaginable terrain. He walked with the gait of a determined outdoor hunter ready to charge over any ground to complete his mission. Edward loved his job almost more than anything else.

When tithe maps were completed in 1841, a shift took place with the firm of Rutherford and Benson. A rail system was on the horizon and Edward's firm had obtained a major contract to survey rail lines in Dorset. This assignment would require Edward to travel and be away from home for extended periods of time.

While Edward loved his wife and daughter, work had a higher priority. To counter his absence Edward took every opportunity to tell young Sarah she was very important and how fortunate he was to have such a wonderful daughter. She basked in the sunshine of his praise. Only later would Sarah realize his praise was placing a not so subtle mantle of responsibility on her shoulders.

WHAT HAPPENED TO MOTHER?

Mrs. Harrison could not believe her daughter Mildred was over twenty-three and not married. From her point of view it would be difficult for a suitor to find another young lady in Shillingstone with a deeper knowledge of domestic skills. She came from a family with a history of hard-working tradesmen and women. Mildred was a handsome woman of medium stature, a matronly countenance, a pleasant personality and a cooperative spirit. Mr. and Mrs. Harrison were more than pleased when Edward Glanville showed an interest in their daughter. Mildred said yes when Edward asked her to marry him, and in the summer of 1836 they were wed.

A year later Mildred informed her husband she was with child. She was anxious as she had little knowledge about giving birth. A midwife assured her that nature would take its course and she would know when the baby was due. With the assistance of Mrs. Mumford, the village midwife, the baby came quickly and Mildred's pain was tolerable. Becoming a mother fulfilled her girlhood dreams and Edward was pleased to have a daughter.

Mildred's mother promised her that when she married she would inherit the family's third generation spinning wheel and baby cradle. She placed baby Sarah in the cradle beside her when she was spinning. If the baby was fussy Mildred would use her left foot to slowly rock the cradle and the right to continue to spin. From her earliest days little Sarah grew up near her mother and her spinning wheel.

Sarah grew from an infant to a darling little girl, adored by her mother. Everything centered on Sarah. She learned to walk before her peers and talked in clear understandable sentences. At an appropriate age her mother taught her domestic skills that had been passed down from her family for generations. Under her mother's tutelage she became exceptional on the spinning wheel. She had a natural dexterity aligning the carded wool in preparation for the spinning wheel. Like her mother she would hum and spin for hours. This energetic young girl would be well-prepared as a future wife and mother as was her mother when she married.

At thirty-eight Mildred was surprised to learn she was expecting another baby. She remembered Sarah's easy birth, but now it felt different. In recent years she had heard horror stories about mothers who died giving birth or shortly afterward. Mildred became obsessed with what might happen when her second baby was born and shared her anxiety with her midwife, Mrs. Mumford. While she had no formal midwife training, Mrs. Mumford had nine children of her own and was well-acquainted with childbirth. Since her birth with Sarah had been normal, Mrs. Mumford suggested this one would likely be the same. It was of little comfort. Not having a doctor in the village increased Mildred's anxiety.

Every Sunday the family attended the village Church of the Holy Rood. Following a morning service Mildred shared her concerns with the vicar and he told her a book of prayers had a particular prayer for mothers giving birth. He indicated it was called, "The Safe Deliverance from the Great Dangers of Childbirth." Both the title and the prayer exacerbated her concern.

As the potential day of delivery grew near, Mildred continued to feel a sense of foreboding. Something was wrong as she felt little movement from her baby. Adding to her tension, Edward was seventy-five miles away in Shrewsbury and would not return for a week. Mildred's fear intensified.

When she had a feeling birth was imminent, Mildred shouted for Sarah to run and get Mrs. Mumford, which she did. On returning they found Mildred on her bed groaning in agony. Mrs. Mumford took charge, telling Sarah, "Child, stoke the fire to heat some water and gather some clean rags." Frightened, Sarah did as she was told. She had never seen her mother in such agony and pain.

Mrs. Mumford said, "Now Mrs. Glanville, push firmly and the baby will come." It didn't come. No part of its head showed. Instead the baby's bottom was displayed. It would be a difficult delivery and it was too late to fetch a doctor. Mrs. Mumford shouted, "Push no more!" She had seen this once before. Fortunately she had brought some salve and soothing oil with her. Carefully she massaged Mildred's tummy in an attempt to turn the baby around. Slowly she felt the baby move on its side. Her massage had achieved a position for delivery.

Eleven-year-old Sarah would no longer wonder how babies were born. She was next to Mrs. Mumford when the head began to show. With her mother bearing down, more of the baby's head appeared. Finally the full head emerged and the rest of the body slid out quickly, in a mixture of mucus, water and blood. It was a boy. As the baby was being washed everyone waited to hear him cry. A cry never came, and he was turning blue. Holding him upside down by his feet, Mrs. Mumford hoped any liquid would drain out. Still no breathing or crying. His color was now deep blue. Suddenly, the baby had a spastic convulsion which almost caused Mrs. Mumford to drop him on the floor. He abruptly gurgled, coughed and cried. An eerie silence was broken by a baby's cry. His cry brought a modicum of joy in the midst of sheer exhaustion.

When the doctor from Blandford arrived the next day he determined the baby had liquid in his lungs. They were not fully developed and might never be. As he lay in his bassinet, every breath was a struggle which contributed to the pallor of his face. He was fragile. Mildred was exhausted, sore and despondent.

A FRAIL CHILD

Absent for the birth of his son, Edward hastily returned home. It had been a traumatic week since the baby had been born. Mildred struggled to explain the baby's bluish color and docile nature. Only grunting sounds and a shallow rattle with irregular breathing greeted Edward. Both parents believed there was a chance the baby might not live very long, but if he did, he would likely be an invalid. They named him Christopher Edward.

The good news for Edward was that his wife was recovering and appeared to be herself once more. Concerned with their son's condition, they soon had him baptized by the vicar in the Church of the Holy Rood. In June of 1848, members and friends gathered to witness the baby's christening. Wearing a white baptismal dress and held by his father, Christopher was quiet and docile while the vicar completed the liturgy of Baptism for the Church of England

Upon returning to their home, Sarah began to realize nothing would ever be the same. Edward returned to work in Shrewsbury and was away for weeks at a time. Before leaving, he reminded Sarah she was a wonderfully capable young daughter and would be of a great help to her mother and baby Christopher. Sarah was warmed by her father's confidence.

At first Mildred doted on her baby boy with the belief that intense love and care would make him normal, but no amount of cuddling, holding, and singing had any effect. He did not improve. There were episodes when he would turn blue and appear on the verge of dying, only to gurgle and cough, with his body convulsing before his breathing would begin once more. For hours he would remain motionless. No amount of a mother's prayers and love helped and it was wearing Mildred down. How could it be that she gave birth to such a beautiful healthy girl and now to an invalid? What did she do to deserve this burden?

During his first year Christopher had only marginal improvement in his breathing. He didn't develop as a normal one-year-old. He was frail, underweight, docile, ate very little and slept frequently. Every breath created a rattle in his lungs. Christopher required little more than basic physical care. As he lay in his bassinet, his very presence placed an immense emotional burden on his mother. While Christopher slept, Mildred did not. She would sit by his cradle near the fireplace, and constantly check to see if he was still breathing. She was being worn down physically and emotionally. After a while she began to lose interest in his care. There were long periods of time she neglected her spinning wheel. Wracked with guilt for giving birth to an invalid, she wondered if it would have been better if he had not survived. Only a tincture of opium calmed her emotions.

With her father gone, with her mother depressed, and with a fragile brother, Sarah was the glue that held the family together. She was exhausted and she was trapped.

A FARMER'S SON

As a young man of eighteen, Byron never missed church on Sunday. It could not have been otherwise. His mother, Kathryn, was the daughter of a vicar and Byron was named after her father, Reverend Byron Chatfield. From the day of his Holy Baptism in the Church of the Holy Rood, his parents took him to church every Sunday. Attending religious services was as important as eating, sleeping or working. Church felt like a second home.

It hadn't always been that way. Howard, a bachelor farmer of thirty five, seldom attended church other than at Christmas and Easter. He was a hard working farmer who had little interest in any maidens in the village or paid much thought to attending church. His work day began at sunrise and ended at sunset. Farming his seven acres was labor intensive with plowing, planting, maintaining, and harvesting. He had little time for anything else.

In 1831 Easter Sunday came on April 3rd and Howard planned to attend the Easter service in the village Church of the Holy Rood. Early in the morning he had bathed, shaved and taken out his Sunday suit, dusted it off, and made sure there were no tears or stains. With a clean shirt and tie he was going to look his best for this holy Easter service.

This year Curate Henry Strickland had invited Reverend Chatfield to deliver the Easter Sermon. The guest minister arrived with his eldest daughter Kathryn, a graceful thirty-two-year old school mistress. As usual the Easter service was well attended and the congregation was buoyed with the Reverend's message that Christ had risen.

At the conclusion of the service, Curate Strickland greeted Howard and told him there was someone he would like him to meet. That someone was Kathryn. The curate knew them both and thought these two single people ought to meet each other. Howard had already noticed the daughter of Reverend Chatfield and had no opposition to being introduced to her. Howard was impressed with Kathryn and she seemed pleased to be introduced to him. It was a meeting that would change both their lives.

Before this time Howard had shown little interest in the female population of Shillingstone and surrounding area, but he was immediately smitten with Kathryn. She was also impressed with Howard as he had an aura of gentle goodness and élan.

The following morning Howard was troubled. He fancied Kathryn but didn't know what to do. He was just a farmer and a vicar's daughter was above his station. What interest would she ever have in him? Farm work kept him busy, but he could not cease thinking about her.

A month later Kathryn sent an invitation to Howard for tea at her father's home in Hinton St. Mary, six miles distant. At this time Reverend Chatfield was an interim vicar for the parish church of St. Peter in the small village of Hinton St. Mary. Howard was astonished, excited and nervous by the invitation. Perhaps she had some interest in him after all. With some help from his pastor, he responded in writing that he would be pleased to accept her invitation. With further correspondence, a date and time were established.

On the appointed day Howard harnessed old Hazel to his trap and steered her toward Hinton St. Mary. To cover six miles Howard estimated it would take an hour and a half with Hazel walking and trotting. The church of St. Peter was next to a large manor home suitable for a wealthy aristocratic family. He was surprised by the size of the rectory and considered turning the trap around and heading back home. But he had promised Kathryn he would come.

He fully expected a servant to open the large front door, but it was Kathryn who greeted him. She welcomed Howard warmly and was not surprised at the puzzled look on his face. When they were seated and comfortably sipping tea, Kathryn told him her father was an interim vicar for the church and they lived in a small area of the manor home. She explained that it had been a nun's residence for the Shaftsbury's Abbey and was now mostly vacant. His anxiety was eased. Kathryn introduced her father, reminding him how they had previously met. When he exited they were alone. Who was going to begin a conversation? They hardly knew each other and his anxiety returned.

In a short time conversation flowed freely between them as though a dam had burst with pent up emotions. Howard was incredulous when she expressed her impressive view of him. Kathryn was receptive to Howard when he expressed his attraction to her when they had first met. They lost track of time and talked for hours. Finally Howard had to leave due to the needs of his farm. They held hands and expressed their mutual joy for the afternoon. Howard didn't want to leave and with hesitation asked, "Do you think your father would allow me to call on you?"

She replied, "Now that you're here, why don't you ask?" In a matter of minutes she brought her father into the parlor, and explained, "Father, Howard has a question for you."

Howard was nervous and felt he was shaking, but he bravely said, "Reverend Chatfield, I would like permission to call on your daughter."

The vicar answered, "Young man, with Kathryn's consent, I would be pleased for you to call on my daughter."

Howard responded, "Thank you, thank you, it will be my honor." With that he looked at Kathryn, smiled, and departed.

Actually, her father was more than pleased that his fussy thirty-two-year old daughter may no longer have the moniker as a spinster.

When Howard awoke the next morning he couldn't remember coming home. His mind was muddled from the events of the previous afternoon. Over breakfast he picked up Kathryn's hand written invitation and read it again. It was real. She was interested in him.

Every other Sunday Howard followed old Hazel to Hinton St. Mary to attend services at the parish church of St. Peter and spend the afternoon with Kathryn. He was besotted with her. Over the next year he courted Kathryn and she responded favorably to this affection. They were in love. Encouraged by her, Howard asked permission from her father to have her hand in marriage and to receive his blessing. Her father happily gave him both. With excitement never before experienced Howard asked Kathryn to marry him and be his wife. She readily responded, "Yes."

Howard had a lot to do. He had inherited a farm that had been in the family for over a hundred and fifty years and a small thatched farmhouse that had changed little over time. It was adequate for the needs of a bachelor farmer, but Kathryn deserved better. Howard decided to build a larger two bedroom timber-framed brick house with an interior of whitewashed wattle and daub walls. It would have a thatched roof and slate floor. He arranged to have the village mason build a large fireplace with a brick oven for the kitchen. He wanted the kitchen to be large enough for a six foot farmer's table. On several occasions Kathryn visited the building in progress, made some suggestions and was pleased with what she saw. It was finished in time for their wedding.

Katherine wanted to be married in the Church of the Holy Rood as it was Howard's home church. Her father agreed to perform the ceremony. In the spring of 1833 a thirty seven year old bachelor and a thirty four year old spinster, exchanged vows and became husband and wife. All who knew Howard and Kathryn were happy for the new couple.

In a short time Kathryn had their farmhouse looking like the home they had envisioned. She quickly stepped into the role of a farmer's wife, helping Howard with the chores, milking the cow and tending the vegetable garden. Howard busied himself with the work of their seven-acre farm. They were deeply in love and enjoyed working together. They eventually developed a rhythm of work on the farm and attendance at church every Sunday.

Many evenings after dinner they would sit at the farm table by the fireplace and Kathryn would introduce him to Bible reading. Conversations on many subjects were new to Howard and he appreciated her interest in expanding his world. At the same time he was mindful that she was educated, socially-experienced, and a vicar's daughter. She was more than he could ever have hoped for. From time to time he wondered what she saw in him as he viewed himself as a simple farmer. Kathryn recognized his candor, his innocent wholesomeness, his motivation to learn and his love for her.

After three years of marriage Katherine informed Howard that he was going to be a father. He could not have been more excited. In the spring of 1836 Kathryn gave birth to a healthy baby boy. They named him Byron after her father and James after Howard's grandfather. Howard was pleased that he had a son who one day would inherit their farm. Kathryn had always wanted to be a mother and committed all her energy and knowledge to the care of little Byron. After dinner Howard would often take Byron in his arms to rock him in front of the fireplace while he read from the Bible until his precious son fell asleep. This was a wonderful new world for both Howard and Kathryn.

Howard noticed that Kathryn was changing. His energetic wife that buzzed around like a busy bee most of the time was slowing down. She became lethargic and rested during the day. Kathryn tried to shrug it off as a temporary feeling and insisted that she would feel better.

In several months she was hardly able to get out of bed. Something was seriously wrong. Howard hitched Hazel to the trap and rushed to Sturminster Newton to fetch the doctor.

In half a day he returned with the doctor who examined Kathryn carefully. He was not able to determine the cause of her lethargy and stomach pain with any certainty. But it was his assumption that she likely had some form of stomach cancer. His conjecture was that she would have three to six months to live. It was shocking news to both of them. He left Kathryn with a bottle of laudanum to ease any suffering and pain and then took his leave. They were in disbelief by what they had been told.

Howard, who had always been attentive to Kathryn, now was solicitous to her every need. He hired help for the farm work so he could spend most of his time with his precious wife. He had no idea what he would do if cancer took her from him. Her suffering became his suffering, her pain became his pain and her courage became his courage. Six months after the doctor had visited Kathryn died.

Howard was devastated. How could such joy bring such sorrow? If it were not for having a three-year-old son, there would have been no purpose to life. When their son was born, their love had been cemented, yet Howard still felt that he had married above his station. He regarded Kathryn as better than himself and believed women should be revered, as being pious, moral and nurturing. She had exemplified all these qualities and when she died, Howard felt he had lost an angel. His father's loving devotion to Kathryn would not be lost on Byron.

Her funeral took place where they first met, the Church of the Holy Rood. Her father Rev. Chatfield conducted the service with great emotion. The church was full with family members and friends of both Kathryn and Howard. She was laid to rest in the cemetery next to the church.

Now the sole care of his three-year-old son was on his shoulders, and it would be impossible to farm and adequately care for him. Fortunately he was surrounded by the congregants of his church. Some of the older ladies made arrangements to care for Byron during the day with Howard managing the remaining time. Prior to her death, Howard had promised Kathryn that he would raise their son just like she would have done and that she would be proud of him as a young man. At an appropriate age, he began to teach Byron to read and write from the pages of the Bible. Church, Bible, farming and the memory of his mother would be the central themes of Byron's early life.

No longer a husband, he was now a grieving widower and single father of his toddler son. He busied himself farming his seven acres. Four acres were plowed and planted with wheat, some rye and oats. Two others were pasture for both work horses and the milk cow. The remaining acre included the farm house and sheds, a pig pen, a hen house, a vegetable garden and some open space. It was a farm he hoped one day would be Byron's, making him the fourth generation of ownership.

When Byron was seven, his father had tilled a small vegetable garden so Byron could plant potatoes, carrots, and onions. After showing him how to plant, it was up to the boy to care for it with watering and weeding. His thoroughness in maintaining the garden provided an abundance of vegetables for the fall and winter season.

As his son was nearing ten, Howard decided he could care for him without the aid of women from the church. He appreciated their help as it had made it possible for Byron to be with him on the farm. He also felt that Byron was old enough to start doing chores such as milking the cow, feeding and watering the horses, pigs and chickens. There was enough work to keep a young boy busy in addition to learning to read and write in the evening hours.

By the time Byron was nineteen he was a fine specimen of a young man. He was six feet tall with a full head of rust-red hair and broad shoulders, muscular arms, proportionate waist, and long powerful legs. He was a handsome young man with pleasant facial features: deep brown eyes, ginger tinted eyebrows, and a firm chin supporting a pleasing smile. The farm now had two farmers, Howard and Byron. There wasn't a job on the farm that the younger man could not handle.

Byron's work on the farm kept him somewhat isolated from the world around him. He had an innocent wholesomeness nurtured by his life on a small farm in a hamlet like Shillingstone. His pleasant manner and grace were inherited from his mother, and from his father he carried a mantle of shyness around young women. Every Sunday at church he was aware of several young women his age, but was too shy to talk to any of them. One of the young women caught his attention and he wanted to know her name, but was too bashful to ask.

That young woman was Sarah Glanville. Young women in the village kept track of eligible young men as there were few, and limited opportunities to meet them. Two places young women and men could meet were at church or a at a village festival. On June ninth, 1855, Shillingstone would hold its Annual Maypole Festival and both Sarah and Byron would be there.

MRS. GERTRUDE HAGGARDY

All across England small villages like Shillingstone celebrated May Day every year on the ninth day of June. Villagers looked forward with anticipation to singing and dancing around their May pole along with many additional festivities. Some years ago the village council had installed an eighty-six-foot pole across Blandford Road from the church grounds. With a population of little more than five hundred, Shillingstone had the bragging rights for the tallest Maypole in Dorset, and likely all of England. Every June ninth this quiet village experienced an explosion in population as hundreds of people from surrounding areas attended their annual May Day festival. However, over time, the event lost some of its excitement. Attendance declined, as little had changed. The pole didn't get taller and events didn't get any better. Those responsible for the festival were in a quandary as to how to revive some enthusiasm and excitement. A solution to their problem would come from an unlikely place, an unlikely person, and an unlikely accident.

Who would have guessed that Bournemouth by the sea, the largest town in Dorset, would contribute to revitalizing the May Day Festival in the small village of Shillingstone? Incredibly the social failure of a Bournemouth woman and the unfortunate death of an elephant trainer would give new life to their fatigued Maypole Festival.

Gertrude Haggardy was a woman with insatiable appetites, physically and socially. Physically she was of generous proportions, and socially, an abject failure.

Gertrude and her husband Milton were an unlikely pair, as he was a six-foot bean pole and she was a five-foot pumpkin. They never failed to draw attention in public.

Milton's calling card read, "Milton Haggardy, Esquire, Attorney at Law." From all indications he had a successful legal practice representing clients of an uncertain reputation. He was a lion in his office, but a kitten at home, where Gertrude reigned supreme. She demanded that Milton help her become accepted in Bournemouth's society. He bought her a large house and had it furnished with the latest style of furniture, paintings, silverware and china. Mrs. Haggardy sent invitations for afternoon tea to the best of Bournemouth society. All turned her down. She sought invitations to social events and received none. Many viewed Gertrude as a crude, loud specimen of womanhood. She had no association with refinement and no amount of window dressing would change the fact that she was a coarse commoner.

A husband who was an attorney had its benefits. Milton researched the history of titles and discovered that centuries earlier, to raise money, the Crown created a category of Baronet so a commoner could purchase a title comparable to a knight. With a payment of 2,000 pounds to the Crown, it was possible to buy the title of Baronet. Milton made the purchase and in a short time a title of Baronet was bestowed on Milton and Gertrude. He was now Sir Milton Haggardy, Baronet and most importantly his wife was now Lady Gertrude Haggardy, Baronetess. Unfortunately a new title was of no avail in opening doors to Bournemouth's society. Sir Milton and Lady Gertrude remained commoners. Gertrude had been called a bombastic hag and was vilified for her audacity to believe she could rise above the status of commoner with a purchased title. A challenge to hereditary aristocracy was reason enough for Gertrude to be censored. A distinction between nobility and commoner was sacrosanct and was the cornerstone of Queen Victoria's realm.

After nine years of marriage Milton died under mysterious circumstances. For years there had been chatter in the legal profession about how Milton had acquired his wealth. It was quite unusual for a solicitor working alone to achieve such financial success. No one was aware of any medical issues and there was no confirmation on the cause of his demise. Some speculated he simply died of natural causes. Others wondered if Gertrude contributed to his death. Perhaps a client was unhappy with his legal representation and did him in. Regardless, his death left Gertrude with substantial assets and cash, contributing to a cloud of suspicion. Lady Gertrude decided she could no longer live in Bournemouth. But where would she go? Gertrude remembered reading of an accident in Shillingstone which involved an elephant and the death of its trainer. The incident had received wide attention in Dorset and beyond. She decided to visit Shillingstone.

Few, if any in Shillingstone had ever heard of Wombwells Menagerie or that it would be passing through their village on the way to Bournemouth with six wagons of exotic animals. One was an African elephant. Few, if any in the area, had ever seen an elephant and the thrill of viewing a real live one was incredible. Unfortunately several days of rain had made Blandford Road slippery with standing pools of water. Villagers called this a "Patten" day. To keep clothes above the mud, many, in particular ladies, wore their shoes attached to a wood board with a wide circular metal ring attached to the bottom. This aided in keeping their clothes and shoes out of the mud.

Word about the coming of an elephant had spread quickly. In anticipation of seeing it the population of Shillingstone had more than doubled. People lined up on both sides of Blandford Road from the entry of the village to the last cottage. Before noon bystanders heard a wailing trumpet sound in the distance. It was the sound of an elephant. As the wagon with the animal entered Shillingstone shouts of excitement and amazement filled the air. A large window with bars on each side of the wagon allowed the elephant to be seen and to flail its trunk around in the air, all the while making high-pitched trumpet sounds. Viewers looked in wonderment at the sight and sound of a real African elephant. As the wagon progressed down Blandford Road it slowed down and stopped in the middle of the village. It was stuck in a rut filled with water. No amount of pulling by team of four horses could free it. The weight of the wagon and elephant made it impossible to move. Four more horses from another wagon were attached, making a team of eight horses. They strained to get the wagon out as the crowd shouted in unison, "pull, pull, pull!" It moved but did not get out of the rut. The horses' handlers decided to give them a rest and water to drink. After a pause the driver cracked a whip and in unison the eight horses jerked the wagon out of the mud. When the trailer lurched, an assistant trainer fell off and slid under the rear wheels. All shouting ceased. Only heavy snorting of exhausted horses could be heard. The man was seriously injured. Klaus, the village blacksmith, offered to carry him to the Old Ox Inn which was accepted and he bent to the task. The unfortunate trainer was placed on a bed and a doctor was requested to attend to the man.

The line of six wagons that had entered Shillingstone in a jubilant atmosphere exited on its way to Bournemouth in reverent silence. It was later reported that the injured man had died four days later. Wombwell's manager made sure that the accident was well covered in all the Dorset newspapers and beyond. This was the story Gertrude remembered reading.

With plans to visit Shillingstone, Gertrude was concerned that her presence would be noticed. She needn't have worried as the village would be crowded with visitors. She arrived the afternoon prior to the Maypole Festival. Her timing was auspicious. For the next several days she saw cheapjack's hawking their wares, parades, Maypole dancing, booths with food and beer, shooting galleries and coconut shies. Moving through the crowd she heard comments about the size of the crowd and complaints about the same events every year. Since she lived in Bournemouth, a seaside tourist destination, she knew what visitors wanted and enjoyed. Gertrude believed she could revitalize the Maypole Festival and find her place in the village of Shillingstone.

First, Gertrude purchased a large house on Church Street near the rectory. As much as she wished to enter Shillingstone unobtrusively, it was not possible. A parade of wagons arrived to fill the house with copious amounts of furniture. After several months, she settled comfortably in her new home. Now her thoughts turned to her place in the village. This dynamo wished to be the queen of her environment and she understood Shillingstone had a vibrant community of tradesmen with few gentry. Gentry be damned, tradesmen would be her path to becoming Shillingstone's queen bee.

A starting point was her neighbor at the rectory, Reverend Edward Arthur Dayman. Gertrude sent a written invitation to the vicar and his wife, Ada, for afternoon tea, which they graciously accepted. At tea, Gertrude assured the vicar of her faith and commitment to the Church of England, and that she would be a faithful communicant in the Church of the Holy Rood. After further pleasantries, she inquired about the Mayday Festival, obtaining as much information as possible. Her offer to help in any way was graciously accepted.

In her first meeting with the Maypole committee, Gertrude sat quietly observing the interaction of committee members. There was an obvious lack of leadership with few ideas about how to improve the festival. She had no intention of making any suggestions right away but for now she would move slowly with her focus being Shillingstone's working men and women.

Gertrude decided to invite the wives of a blacksmith, a baker, a mason and postmaster for afternoon tea. Such an occurrence was unheard of. Prior to sending formal invitations, Gertrude asked the vicar's wife if she would be willing to explain the appropriate etiquette for afternoon tea. Ada indicated that she would be delighted to meet with the wives at the church rectory. Gertrude's invitation included information that the vicar's wife would explain tea etiquette.

Gertrude created quite a stir of excitement with the four women. None had ever received an invitation for afternoon tea or really knew anything about it. All accepted. When they met at the rectory, Ada was flooded with questions. She explained how to hold a delicate tea cup, adding sugar, tea, and milk in that order. There was also a proper way to stir the cup. Rather than stir in a circle, the spoon was to be moved gently back and forth between the 6 and 12 o'clock position. No one had the courage to ask why. Likely there wasn't an answer. Afternoon tea would include finger sandwiches and scones. All were apprehensive, yet excited about the event.

Perhaps more important than tea was what to wear. Normally village women would only have a dress for Sunday. All agreed they needed a new frock. The dress shop on Blandford Road had a rush of activity as four wives were in the market for stylish new clothes. Selecting a dress for the right price was more difficult than imagined. Fabrics, colors, styles, accessories, and bonnets were all a challenge. Working together they each selected an outfit that would be appropriate for afternoon tea. Other village wives were envious, but were assured by Gertrude that their turn would come.

In upper society, conversation during afternoon tea usually turned to gossip, but Gertrude had a different agenda. She wanted to be accepted by her guests. Afternoon tea would simply be an opportunity to become acquainted. If she could not be accepted by the upper class in Bournemouth, she believed she could be accepted by the hard working men and women along Blandford Road.

Since a villager rarely travelled more than ten miles from home, Gertrude was sure that none would have heard about the mysterious death of her husband or that she had left Bournemouth under a cloud of suspicion. No such ignorance could be assured from the landed gentry. Travel had few limitations for England's aristocracy. Gossip seemed to be a coin of society and its impact significant. Gertrude's concern about what had happened in Bournemouth was justified.

There was little discourse between tradesmen and gentry other than church on Sunday or community festivals. One bridge of communication between the two classes was the Church and the vicar Reverend Edward Dayman. He was about to be caught in the middle of an issue concerning Gertrude Haggardy. One of the largest landowners in Shillingstone, Lord Richard Hatfield, representing the gentry, asked the Reverend to look into the presence of Mrs. Haggardy from Bournemouth. Some in society were concerned that she would be as troublesome in their village as she had been in her former one. They would prefer that she move on.

Unknown to Lord Hatfield, Reverend Dayman had welcomed Gertrude to Shillingstone. He believed she would be a benefit for the majority of the villagers and had publicly expressed support for her leadership. Ada was also supportive. Was there a problem? When asked, Lord Hatfield questioned the legitimacy of her title as Lady Haggardy. Historically the title of Baronet was legitimate, but no longer. Lord Hatfield wished this gritty bombastic woman would be exposed as a fraud. As spokesman for the landed gentry, he requested that the Reverend Burton address the problem. She was like an irksome sliver in the finger of the nobility.

As vicar, Reverend Dayman's position in Queen Victoria's England was unique. After training and ordination he became an employee of the Church of England with the Queen as Head of the Church. While he ministered to every member of his congregation, he socialized with the gentry, and they viewed him as one of their own. Reverend Dayman had been vicar since 1842 and was beloved by his parish. He sincerely viewed his position as a spiritual calling. Lord Hatfield's request put him in a difficult position where he would need to have the Wisdom of Solomon and the patience of Job. Fortunately he had both. Reverend Dayman assured Lord Hatfield he would address his lordship's concerns and recommend a resolution amenable to all parties. Reverend Dayman decided to wait until Gertrude had afternoon tea with her four guests. Nothing like this had ever happened, and many villagers were excited to have a report when it was over.

On the appointed afternoon four ladies, dressed in their finest, arrived at the home of Lady Gertrude. If they had ever wondered what the inside of a wealthy person's home looked like, they wondered no more. It was elegant. Gertrude welcomed them warmly with a handshake and a maid directed them to the parlor to be seated. Lady Gertrude complimented them on their dresses and how beautiful they looked. At close to three hundred pounds, Gertrude dressed as best she could. She wore an off-white cotton muslin dress with a high waist to support her ample bosom. It had short puffy sleeves showing puffy arms, puffy hands and dimpled fingers. A sash under her bust gave some support and a pleated skirt flowed to the floor with enough material for a tent.

Finally all were seated around a well-appointed table for tea. Nervously the ladies demonstrated the etiquette learned from Ada. After their first cup of tea they relaxed and began to chatter as though this was something they had done every afternoon. Gertrude asked about their husbands, their children and their daily activities. She was complimentary toward each of the wives. As a side benefit, the women learned much about each other. Gertrude shared a little about her life, the death of her husband and the fact that he had provided for her adequately. Before tea was over Gertrude indicated that she looked forward to their friendship and she would like to be a benefit to the community. All were pleased. In the glow of afternoon tea Gertrude was unaware she was about to face a crisis.

Several days after her event, a note arrived from the vicar Dayman requesting a visit at her earliest convenience. Why? Likely he wanted to thank her for hosting tea for ladies of the parish. She was happy to accept his invitation

When Gertrude arrived at the rectory, Reverend Burton thanked her for her social event with the wives of local tradesmen. Then he came straight to the point. He informed her in detail of Lord Hatfield's concern and his Lordship's wish that she should leave Shillingstone. For the first time in her life Gertrude was shocked and speechless. He was so blunt she was shocked her mouth opened and she began to fidget in her chair. It was a response the vicar anticipated. Now they talked. He pointed out the landed gentry of Shillingstone were displeased and objected to her vulgar personality and her claim to be a Baroness. Her claim was a threat to their inherited nobility and a violation of their social sensibilities. After what seemed like a long pause, he had a recommendation.

While Reverend Dayman was a minister, he was also a mediator. He had one foot in the upper social order and the other with village workers. He gave her his suggestion. She should state that she had no interest in a social relationship with the landed gentry and would not use her title. He further pointed out that she could be an asset to the working community of the village, as illustrated by her afternoon tea. The event had become a wonderful experience for the women. For the first time in her life Gertrude realized her energy could be used to help others and as a result, she could establish an important position for herself in the community. All parties to this crisis accepted Reverend Dayman's counsel. Gertrude felt freed from the shadow that followed her from Bournemouth. Curiously, the social order she had overlooked in Bournemouth serendipitously embraced her in Shillingstone.

Gertrude continued to have her afternoon tea with the local women. As a result some of them decided to have tea among themselves, with amended etiquette. Now in addition to Sunday services, they had another reason to dress up. None of this excitement was lost on the proprietor of the dress shop or on a few husbands who discovered the benefits in having happy wives. Afternoon tea created a new social dynamic and a positive identity for the working class of Shillingstone. With renewed energy Gertrude set out to chair the Maypole Festival committee and make it an event that would be memorable for years to come.

A BLACKSMITH

It had been six months since the village blacksmith had died and the ashes from his forge had long ago turned cold. Acrid smoke no longer wafted over the village. During this time Shillingstone's villagers had to travel five miles in either direction for the services of a blacksmith. The distance was untenable. The Parish Council realized their village without a blacksmith was like a wagon without wheels. They had urgent meetings to find another smithy without success. Since 1842 Shillingstone had a telegraph office which provided communication with most of England, but no one on the council knew how or whom to contact. They resorted to inter-village gossip requesting leads in search of a blacksmith. They were surprised by the response.

About this time a couple had recently escaped from the warring factions in Austria. Klaus Oberdorf was a large man and a skilled blacksmith who was about to be conscripted into the Austrian army where foot soldiers had a short life expectancy. He and his wife, Helga, escaped from Austria through Germany, France and then to England. In London they found a German emigrant community where they were accepted and could communicate in their own language.

An individual in this community learned that a village called Shillingstone needed a blacksmith. He sent a telegram to the village council and recommended Klaus Oberdorf, an experienced and highly skilled blacksmith. The council questioned if he could speak English. The answer was no. They had a choice between two candidates. One was skilled and spoke no English, the other was an English man with undefined smithing skills. The parish council met and decided to accept Klaus, hoping he would learn the native tongue. Within a week Klaus and Helga arrived in Shillingstone with all their worldly possessions stuffed in a cloth travel bag. They were warmly welcomed in sign language. Before going to their accommodations, Klaus had to see the forge. On seeing the mess, his eyebrows and forehead were raised, but his face broke into a broad smile at the potential.

It was only a few days until the forge was billowing out its usual noxious smoke as Klaus attacked raw iron on his anvil, making new tools and repairing the old ones. A language barrier did not hinder him from making what villagers needed and they were always finished on time. Soon Klaus began to understand English words and he would respond with, "Vat u vant? Ya, Ya, I do."

Klaus was huge! No man in Shillingstone equaled his girth and height. His arm muscles were enormous and with one hand he could pick up a water cask. Beneath his well-worn leather apron was a chest like a barrel of flour and his legs looked like tree trunks. Years hammering on an anvil had developed the strength few man would achieve. How strong was Klaus? It was rumored he was as strong as an ox.

Stories of Klaus's strength and kindness were legion. When he heard that Mrs. Sower's sow had escaped its pen and was stuck in a mud puddle, he came to her rescue. Others had tried to free the sow, but a squealing and wiggling six hundred pounds made it impossible. He had no difficulty finding Mrs. Sower or the pig as it was squealing in a panic and her owner was screaming in distress. After viewing the scene, Klaus, with his leather apron and all, stepped into the mud, put his arms under the sow and lifted her out of her bed of mud. A surrounding crowd cheered at this marvelous rescue. Finally the pig was back in its pen and 16 chirping little piglets were delighted to have their food supply returned.

At Shillingstone's annual Maypole Festival, Klaus annually challenged men of the village to a rope pull. At first it was five men against Klaus and they quickly lost. Then ten men tried and lost. Someone shouted, "Klaus, you couldn't beat an ox."

Klaus replied, "Bring the ox."

A harness was attached to an ox and then another to Klaus at the opposite end of the rope. When a flag dropped, the ox was whipped and bellowing loudly. Tried to move but only dug up dirt and dust. Both ox and Klaus were sweating profusely but there was little movement for ten minutes. Finally Klaus decided to end the contest and pulled the snorting beast backward over the line. Exhausted, the ox lapped a pail of ale and a weary Klaus guzzled his mug of lager. More stories could be told, but to continue might question their credibility.

For as long as anyone could remember, the blacksmith's smithy was next to the Post Office. Villagers often passed to stop and watch Klaus work magic by pounding iron on his anvil. It was not a large shop but it had three walls with a slanted roof, front to back. His front wall was four feet high with the rest of the wall hinged at the top to provide shade during the day and lowered to close the shop at night. The most important item of the workshop was the fire of the forge and bellows to increase the fire's temperature. A large anvil sat atop a big block of wood and next to it a slack tub of water. These three items sitting on a dirt floor allowed Klaus to be a successful smithy. All three walls were covered with a menagerie of tools such as tongs, files, and hammers, forms to make nails, metal sheers and an abundance of tools of his trade.

Farm horses plodded over fields pulling a metal plow, with horse shoes made by Klaus. He made tools for planting and scythes for harvesting. In addition he made hinges, axes, spades, and hundreds of nails. If an item could be described Klaus could make it. Those who stopped by his shop seemed to enjoy the sights, sounds and smells of his forge. For Klaus the smell assured him that he was making a good living.

A MAYPOLE FESTIVAL

Through the late fall and into early 1855, Gertrude guided the Maypole committee to complete their plans and objectives for the annual festival. When formed, their plan required many volunteers. A call for helpers was announced and the response was overwhelming. A major preparation was maintenance on the eighty-six foot pole. A scaffold was built to inspect a large wheel atop the pole. It would take the better part of a day using the skills of the village carpenter, the blacksmith and six strong young men. Byron volunteered to be one of the six men. Farm work had given him a chiseled muscular physique. It was a hot sunny day and in no time the hard working young men's sweat-soaked shirts were removed. A bevy of young beauties tried unsuccessfully not to notice. Their assignment was to prepare long ribbons to hold garlands of flowers. The distraction of these bare chested young men made it difficult.

Unbeknownst to one another, Byron and Sarah had volunteered to work on the same day. Byron worked on the scaffold at the base of the Maypole, while nearby Sarah prepared ribbon lengths. While they had seen each another in church and around the village, they had never spoken. Finally they were close to each other and Sarah took the lead and introduced herself, after which Byron quietly responded with his name. For the next several days they worked together, smiling and laughing. A mutual attraction developed between them and Byron's shyness began to fade. After preparations on the Maypole concluded, Sarah took a bold step and asked Byron if he would be her escort for the festival. Surprised and almost speechless, he smiled and told her it would be his honor.

As the festival day approached, an aura of excitement filled the air. While the fair started on Saturday, June ninth, other activities began days earlier. From early morning to late evening Blandford Road was jammed with peddlers hawking their wares. They were selling pots, pans, fruits, vegetables, sweets, beverages and medicine that supposedly had miraculous curative benefits. None refused the opportunity to sell products to throngs of people anxious to be part of the coming festival. For the first time space on the festival ground had been set aside for ten cheapjack families to park their wagons and sell their wares. They set up booths, tents, and tables to display and market their products. Celebrations of this nature were never overlooked by those who had goods to sell.

Early Saturday morning crowds were milling up and down Blandford Road anxious for the Maypole Festival parade to begin. Mixing with the crowd, early peddlers and cheapjack's hawked their wares and began shouting out the benefit of what they had to sell, *"A bargain, a bargain, buy before all the pots and knives are gone!"*

Sturminster Newton's brass band assembled on the grounds of the church rectory and created a booming cacophony of musical sound as members warmed up their brass instruments in preparation for the parade. A short distance away Blandford Forum's fife and drum corps arrived and were warming up their fifes, testing their snare drums and pounding on their bass drum. Piercing sounds of whistling fifes floated through the air and snare drummers used keys to adjust their instruments for just the right tone. A large group of villagers of all ages blew their tin whistles which filled the air with their shrill high-pitched disorganized sounds. Others waved colorful banners and flags of all shapes and sizes in practice for the parade. The excitement was contagious.

At midmorning the vicar, dressed in his ecclesiastical vestments, stepped out of the rectory to the middle of the yard and raised his pastoral staff to boisterous cheers from the gathered crowd. With this signal the parade began.

A short distance down Church Street in front of her house, Gertrude Haggardy was waiting to take her place at the end of the parade. She had rented an open royal blue landau carriage with gold trim, with a uniformed driver and two beautiful white prancing horses.

Marching in formation and playing the "The British Grenadiers," the Sturminster Newton brass band led the annual Maypole parade. Crowds on each side of Blandford Road waved and cheered when they heard the inspiring music. A short distance behind came Vicar Dayman waving and blessing the crowd. Church members followed, with flapping banners displaying symbols of past saints of the church. Next Blandford Forum's fife and drum corps stepped lively as they played the fast paced energetic martial song, "Old Towler." Shouts and clapping from the bystanders cheered them on. A short distance behind, villagers with tin whistles blew with all the energy they could muster.

Then came the climax: Gertrude Haggardy appeared in her open carriage dressed in her finest clothing and white kidskin gloves, typical of a queen, with two white high-stepping horses pulling her carriage up Blandford Road. It looked like royalty had come to Shillingstone. A little child in the crowd shouted, "It's the queen, it's the queen!" Those around her laughed as her mother smiled and patted the child on the head. Gertrude could not have been happier. She was the "Queen" of Shillingstone.

When the parade was over, several thousand visitors were eager to experience all that the festival had to offer, some excessively. There was a variety of booths selling sweets, toys, food and beer. As usual there was a rush to the booth selling beer. The shooting gallery was as popular as ever. Young ladies knew this was where young men could be found. Few owned a gun and it was exciting to experience shooting a rifle. Mixed in were family cheapjacks putting on a show to gain interest in their wares. Card games were popular and quick money for a cheapjack. One huckster made good money in a shell game. In front of their tents fortune tellers shouted out, "The parson can tell you about the afterlife, I can tell you about your present life!"

Young men and women from small villages like Shillingstone had few opportunities to meet and the annual Maypole celebration became the best opportunity to mingle. A popular meeting place was the Coconut Shire Booth. Here coconuts were placed on top of a pole and the contestant had to knock one off by throwing a small hard ball. It cost a farthing for three balls. However few succeeded. Sarah looked at Byron and said, "Why don't you try, you're a strong young man." It was a challenge and how could he refuse? He paid his farthing and missed all three times.

Looking at Sarah he said, "Maybe it's not strength after all." Miffed and a little embarrassed, he paid for three more balls. His first ball again missed the target. Now Byron took his time. Sarah was watching intently with her body leaning forward to give him nonverbal encouragement. He had only two balls left and he was pressured to knock the coconut over. He didn't want to disappoint Sarah or himself. With ball in hand he reached back, intently looking at the target and threw the ball. It was close but again missed. This was turning out to be more difficult than he thought. He looked at Sarah and declared, "This is harder than it looks, but here goes!" With that he took the last little ball and threw it with every ounce of strength in his body and the ball hit the coconut square on, but it didn't fall. He had hit it so hard liquid leaked out. When the owner saw the situation he swiftly kicked the post and the coconut fell to the ground.

Sarah jumped up and down squealing, "You did it, you did it!" She looked at Byron, opened her arms and gave him a spontaneous hug. Byron was surprised he had hit the target and by Sarah's response. He enjoyed both. His prize was a coconut.

Klaus Oberdorf, the village blacksmith, challenged anyone to beat him in a tug-of-war. Local stories about his strength were legion. Everyone in the village had heard about the time Mrs. Sower's six-hundred-pound-pig escaped its pen and got stuck in a mud puddle and how Klaus, lifting the sow single-handedly, came to its rescue. Knowing his reputation, not a single man would take his challenge, not two or even four. Eventually ten men came together to challenge him, and the contest was on. After going back and forth, with groans and shouts and cheers from by-standers, no one was winning. A crowd grew to watch and cheer, some for the challengers, a few for Klaus. But neither the men nor Klaus could win so the contest was declared a tie. All were gasping for breath and dripping with sweat when Klaus roared, "Beer for all."

Moving through the crowd, Byron and Sarah saw a group of children lined up for a footrace and noticed that some young people were preparing for a three-legged race. Byron looked at Sarah and asked her to be his partner. She sheepishly agreed. Like the other young women Sarah tied the lower half of her dress in a knot to be able to race with Byron. Like the other girls Sarah tied her right leg to his left leg and Byron put his arm around her waist, they were ready. At the start it was awkward and funny as couples fell. Sarah was about to fall when Byron picked her up with his arm around her waist and carried her over the finish line where they collapsed. Even though they cheated, it was fun. Still tied together, they lay on the ground out of breath, facing each other laughing hysterically. It was a magic moment they would not forget.

All during the day groups of children and young girls danced around the Maypole. Fife and fiddle players provided tunes suggesting the style of dance. As they moved around the pole, some children went in and out and around each other, then they would reverse their direction. Many girls wore beautiful white dresses and colorful ribbons and flowers in their hair. It was a beautiful sight and sound to behold. Dancing continued all day long.

Sarah stood listening to the music and the gaiety of the dancers, and she was excited to be with Byron. But the time came when she had to be home to meet her family responsibilities. They left the festival grounds hand in hand on their way to Sarah's home. Byron escorted her to her front door. As she turned to thank him, Byron put his arm around her waist and pulled her close as she gave him a kiss on his cheek. Neither wanted to let go. Sara knew it was a day she would long remember. Byron whistled all the way back to the farm. Sarah heard his whistle as he left.

Sarah never told Byron the difficulty she had to get a full day away from home. When she entered the door her father told her he was displeased that he had to care for his wife and annoyed that he could not leave when he wished. Sarah's happy day was spoiled by her father's words.

In her home on Church Street, Gertrude could hear the music and noise of the revelers. For the first time she was content with her life and knew she had found a home.

A BEGINNING

Byron and Sarah were fortunate to have discovered each other. Living in a small village with little mobility made finding someone of the opposite sex difficult. Choices and opportunities were few. Some young people found a match in church or at a village festival. It was during Shillingstone's Maypole Festival that Byron and Sarah experienced the freedom to be with each other and make a connection. Like most young couples in rural communities they were not restrained by courtship guidelines of the nobility, of which they had little knowledge and many parents had little influence in a decision in whom a young person could or would marry.

In the weeks after the festival, Sarah and Byron saw each other as much as possible. With Byron's horse and trap they took rides through the countryside around Shillingstone. Under a canopy of trees on the banks of the River Stour, they stopped in an open space with a pleasant view. Sarah had prepared a picnic basket and decided this was the perfect place to enjoy its contents. It was a wonderful location to relax and get to know each other. Sarah was impressed by Byron's warm personality and pleasing manners. He was handsome and she loved his bushy red hair. She was excited by being with him. Neither was in a hurry to leave this romantic spot.

Byron noticed that Sarah had been looking at him and asked, "What are you looking at?"

She replied, "You." Sarah continued, "I am so happy to be here with you and feel like I could stay here forever."

"I don't know what to say, except I feel the same." More than once Byron had thought how fortunate he was to have met her at the May Day festival. He was happy to be sitting beside her in this beautiful place. He enjoyed her perky personality, her beauty, and her dimples when she smiled, which was often. They were in no hurry to leave.

After they had eaten, Byron wanted Sarah to meet his father. She pleasantly agreed. When they arrived at the farm, Sarah immediately loved the open space, the sound of bleating sheep and the smell of fresh-cut grass. She was impressed with Byron's father. Straightaway the feeling was mutual. Even shaking his strong, rough farmer's hand was pleasant. For a fleeting moment, in this open space, Sarah felt free from the confinement and responsibilities that awaited her at home.

It was difficult for Sarah to get free from home. One evening she was able to spend some time at the Old Ox Inn, sharing Byron's beer and tapping her foot to the music of a local group. Sarah was looking for love and watching Byron, she could not believe she might have found it. Byron was not looking for love, but love had found him. It was a magic moment. Both realized what was happening. Two young people were in the throes of their first love. Excitedly they talked about their past. Sarah shared the excitement of being a young girl and having fun with her girlfriends. Those were happy days. Byron shared about growing up on a farm and learning about horses, pigs and all the work involved in keeping weeds out of his turnip field. He enjoyed it all. Conversation about the past was pleasing, but they were slow to speak about the future.

Sarah did not share with Byron the full extent of responsibility her father had placed on her to care for her mother and Christopher. When he was away, which was often, Sarah was the total caregiver for them both. When her father was home he wanted his freedom to leave the cottage whenever he wished. Sarah's only temporary relief was a neighbor woman who helped occasionally. It was her burden and she did not want it to affect her relationship with Byron.

Summer was nearly over and autumn was upon them. For Byron the harvest was over, but for Sarah nothing had changed. Her mother's emotional status was unpredictable. Christopher continued to be fragile. Sarah had introduced Byron to her family, but her father showed little interest in her excitement concerning the young man. Edward continued to remind Sarah she was the best daughter a father could ever have, and he praised her for caring for her mother and Christopher.

In contrast Byron's father felt differently. Howard was prepared to give his blessing for any decision the couple would make. He thought they made a wonderful pair.

It was time. Sarah knew it was coming and was apprehensive. In the coolness of the fall Sarah and Byron were wrapped in a blanket against the cold when they took a ride in the country to their favorite picnic area on the banks of the Stour River. Bundled up in the blanket and sitting in the trap everything was different. Most of the trees were void of leaves and cool winds were blowing around where they sat. Byron tried his best to talk and turned to Sarah and said, "Sarah, I have never been in love before now. From the time we have been together I have grown to love you with all my heart and am asking you to be my wife."

With tears of joy she responded, "Byron, my Byron, I do love you and want to marry you and be your wife more than anything. I want to say yes right now, but it would be difficult. I have responsibilities at home that I need to resolve. I would be thankful if you could give me a few days to address my issues at home."

Her response was not what Byron had expected. What could he say? After a pause, he agreed to wait. Silently they cuddled in the cold for a little while. Then Byron took her home.

Sarah was desperately trying to find a way to solve her dilemma, but could not. The man she thought she would never find was right in front of her. She had questioned whether she would ever experience such love, and she believed she had found it. At the same time three other people she loved depended on her, two for their very survival. She was torn between her love for Byron and an obligation to her family. If she turned down Byron's proposal, would she ever get another? Would this be her only chance to have a family of her own? She was not sure what her father would say and it was not possible to reach him. After two sleepless nights and a great amount of anxiety, she decided she would accept Byron's proposal of marriage, but ask for time to settle matters at home without knowing how long that would take. She was worried how Byron would respond.

Waiting was just as difficult for Byron. After years of listening to his father's elevated view of women, in particular his mother Kathryn, he could not help being influenced into thinking the same about Sarah. She reminded him of the wonderful caring qualities he believed were in his mother. He was the son of a farmer and Sarah was the daughter of an educated surveyor. Like his father, Byron wondered if he would be marrying above his station. Would she find him worthy of being her husband?

Several days later they met at the Old Ox Inn. They sat at a table in a quiet corner near the fireplace with a sense of uncertainty. Sarah was exhausted and nervous as she spoke. "Byron, I love you with all my being. I never thought I would ever meet and love such a wonderful man as you. Yes, I want to marry you and to have you as my husband, but I need some time to resolve some of my family responsibilities and I'm not sure how long that will take."

Byron was not prepared for what Sarah said. He had been thinking of a wedding in the Church the Holy Rood in front of all their family and friends. Now he silently tried to think of words to respond. He sat pensively with his elbows on the arms of his chair, his hands clasped together with both index fingers across his lips while he stared into space. He was deep in thought. He wondered if Sarah's family was more important than their love for each other. He loved her deeply and could not conceive of loving another. She did say yes and he knew she was worth waiting for. Finally he responded, "Sarah, I love you more than anyone in the world and look forward to having you as my wife. I accept your decision and I am willing to wait." Without any serious aforethought, he impetuously continued, "I would find it difficult to walk the streets of Shillingstone knowing that I could not be with the woman I love. I do not know where or when I will go or what I will do, but I cannot remain in Shillingstone." Sarah was startled and puzzled. What did he mean?

With her head in a whirl she excused herself and went home feeling apprehensive about their future. Byron remained at the table near the fireplace massaging his beer and also feeling confused. What had he just done? He was befuddled and sat in silence for some time. An older gentleman noticed his isolation and apparent distress. With a military bearing, and a pint in his hand, he moved toward Byron and sat down next to him. It took a moment for Byron to realize someone was near. The gentleman said, "Young man you look troubled. Can I freshen your pint?"

Byron's answer came slowly, "Yes...yes...thank you." After introductions and a second beer, Byron opened up about his situation to a crusty retired sergeant from the India Bengal Horse Artillery. They talked for what seemed like hours. Sergeant Clarence Wilson regaled Byron with his adventures in the military during the British wars in India. The young man was transfixed and listened to dramatic stories and acts of heroism. He wondered if they were still accepting recruits. Sergeant Wilson assured him there was never a time they were not recruiting.

Returning to the farm, Byron told his father everything that had happened. Howard was pleased that Sarah had accepted his son's proposal, but disappointed about an indefinite delay. Byron also told him about meeting Sergeant Wilson and the possibility of joining the Bengal Horse Artillery. Howard was alarmed about the implications of such a decision, but was supportive. Byron said he would have to enlist for seven years, a long time to be away from Sarah.

When Byron said he could not stay in Shillingstone he had given no thought to where he would go or what he would do. It was an impulsive statement, but it was how he felt. Now the only choice he knew was a suggestion from Sergeant Wilson. If he left home Byron would be going to an unknown place in an unknown world surrounded by unknown people, for seven years. Taking a step in that direction could be considered courageous or utterly foolish. He hoped it would not be the latter.

His father had a story to tell him. Having been married to the daughter of a vicar, he was familiar with Scripture. He told Byron the tale of Laban, Jacob and Rachel from the book of Genesis. Jacob wanted to marry his love, Rachel, but lacked a dowry. Her father, Laban, told Jacob if he worked seven years for him, he could have Rachel as his wife. The story continued that he worked for seven years which seemed like only a few days because he loved her deeply. Aware the story was more complicated, Howard decided this would suffice. Over the next several days Byron made the decision to join the army and sign up for the required period of seven years.

A week later Byron met Sarah at her cottage and confirmed his decision to leave Shillingstone. She had hoped he would change his mind. She asked, "Where are you going to go?"

Byron replied, "I met a retired soldier at the Old Ox Inn and he recommended joining the army and that's what I am going to do."

"When are you leaving? How long will you be gone?"

"I'll be leaving in a few days and I will be gone for seven years."

Sarah was momentarily silent in utter shock and then cried out, "You can't, that's forever!" She was shaking when he held her and said he would love her always. She never imagined it would be seven years. With difficulty she replied, "That's an eternity." There was nothing more to be said.

Joining the army meant the possibility he could be wounded or killed. That stark realization came like a flash of lightening. She might never see him again. For the next several days her mind was muddled. She slept little and felt despondent about the future. Sarah realized she had put family loyalty above her love of Byron. She was frightened and murmured with no one listening, "What have I done?"

CAMP ALDERSHOT

Byron had never been more than ten miles beyond his father's farm and he was now going into the unknown for the next seven years. After saying his goodbye to Sarah, he decided to visit Sergeant Wilson, a resident at the Old Ox Inn. He wanted to know what lay ahead. In the months to come he would discover innocence was not an asset in the world he was about to enter.

He found Sergeant Wilson with his usual pint near the fireplace. "Sir, I have decided to join the artillery you talked about the last time we met, but where can I go to join up?"

Sergeant Wilson replied, "There's a new military camp at Aldershot, just outside a village of the same name and it would be a journey of about two days."

Byron continued to bombard him with all kinds of questions, which he succinctly answered. Byron's final question was, "What clothes should I take?"

Smiling, the sergeant responded, "The clothes on your back and an extra pair of underpants. Everything else will be provided."

After bouncing around in a coach for two days, Byron finally arrived at Camp Aldershot. He was about to experience the rough and tumble world of a new recruit in the British army. On arrival he found his way to the recruiting office where he explained he wanted to join the army and be part of the Bengal Horse Artillery. The recruiter was puzzled when Byron wanted to sign up only for the Bengal Horse Artillery. No such a regiment existed at Aldershot, so the recruiter put him on the list to be a British foot soldier and told him he would be in training for the next six months. This was not what Sergeant Wilson told him to expect.

In short order he was given all the equipment he would need, from a uniform to a canteen bottle. He was then assigned to a barracks with twenty-five other recruits. When Byron arrived at his barracks he was greeted by a well-worn middle aged soldier who said he was Corporal Frazer in charge of all recruits and he emphatically announced, "From this day forward my name will no longer be Corporal Frazer, it will be Sir!" Outside the barracks he stood the men in two lines and told them the facts of life in the British army. He alone would tell them when to wake up, when to sleep, when to eat, when to talk and when to use the latrine. They could expect that any deviation from his orders would bring harsh punishment. Then he disclosed what they could look forward to in training during the next six months. It did not appear pleasant.

Byron looked at his fellow recruits and saw an unruly group of men. Several were young, but most were older and looked like they had lived a hard life. He later learned some had been gang pressed, some had been drunks, several had been criminals, and two were former deserters. Others joined who had lost jobs from a factory or mill. Byron and another young man were the only recruits who were farmers' sons. In the midst of these miscreants Byron felt he may have made a wrong decision. Regardless, he was now a recruit about to become a foot soldier in Her Majesty's service.

For the first time in his life Byron was stuck in a group of troublemakers. Absent the corporal, discord and rabble-rousing was rampant. Without a leader there was constant conflict and Byron determined that needed to change. He used his height and strong voice to shout to get their attention. Byron had never done this before and surprised himself, but he believed the situation required it. With a commanding voice he told them someone in the barracks had to be in charge to settle differences among them. He stood tall and confidently asked, "Are there any volunteers?" Other than the sound of shuffling feet, there was silence. After a pause he firmly said, "Then I will accept that position, unless there is any disagreement." There was no objection. They assumed this tall strong son of a farmer, could whip any one of them if one would choose to try. Byron had never thought of himself as a leader of men but at this moment he was.

Discipline was paramount. Recruits were taught the basics of army life, the history of battles, marching, marching and more marching. At a shooting range they were shown how to shoot and care for their Enfield-Pattern 1853 rifles. Foot soldiers were taught to stand in rigid lines two or three deep without faltering. They were ordered to stand their ground and wait until the enemy was close, fire their muskets, then charge with fixed bayonets. When faced with a ferocious bayonet attack, many enemy soldiers would rapidly retreat. After six months of intense training they were assigned to the sixth light infantry regiment of the British army.

In spite of many challenges Byron began to relish army life, but not as a foot soldier. During the months at Aldershot, Byron wrote to Sergeant Wilson and told him he had not been assigned to the Bengal Horse Artillery and needed his help. After several letters between Sergeant Wilson and the base commander Byron was at last approved for transfer to the Bengal Horse Artillery. It would not be easy.

Already there was a problem. Byron would have to leave England and sail to India, as the Bengal Horse Artillery regiment was based in Calcutta. He would need to sail halfway around the world to the Dum Dum Military Garrison, a short distance from Calcutta. Still not knowing where it was located, Byron confirmed that was where he wanted to go.

Several years of a cholera epidemic had reduced the India Bengal armed forces by ten percent and new recruits were urgently needed. Byron's timing could not have been better. There existed a quasi-relationship between the British military and the Bengal army in India, and passage was provided for him.

Byron was assigned to a temporary army facility in London with thirty-seven other recruits bound for India. Fortunately a Man-of-War would soon be sailing with provisions and ammunition for the Bengal armed forces. Several days prior to sailing, Byron and five other recruits decided to tour London. He was shocked at what he saw. London was a large dirty city with foul-smelling manure in the streets and more horses than people. Everywhere they went they were harassed by peddlers, street urchins and prostitutes. Back at their barracks Byron thought about the incredible contrast between London and his peaceful farm back home. He decided to write Sarah prior to leaving England.

Dear Sarah: On many evenings while resting on my bed, I have thought of the wonderful times we had together. I love you very much and miss you already. I have been told that I will board a ship for India in a couple of days and I want you to know where to send your letters. Mail them to Camp Aldershot and they will forward them to where I am located. Basic training was a challenge, but I completed all the courses. It may be many months before I receive any of your letters in India. I wish I could be with you and tell you of my love for you. Your loving Byron

All thirty-seven recruits were ordered to pack their gear and be ready for a trip to the Portsmouth Naval Yard the next morning. A trip of two days brought them to the sprawling Portsmouth Naval Yard with ships of every variety, some at anchor, others tethered to a quay filled with a variety of cargo, with stevedores scurrying to fill the hold of a large sailing ship. It was here they stopped and with their gear they were led to a half empty cargo building. Waiting for them was the First Officer of the ship they were to board for India. After they gathered around him, he introduced himself and asked a question, "Gentlemen have any of you sailed abroad before?"

They looked nervously at each other and unanimously said, "No."

"Then here are the rules you will need to follow. You will be assigned to the same lower deck as the ship's crew but in a separate area. You will be treated no better or no less than the regular jack-tar. You will not be involved with the operation of the ship. You will keep your quarters in order and clean. Weather permitting, you may have no more than five men on the deck at a time and will not hinder the operation of the crew. Any questions?" There was silence. "Then you may spend a little time on the quay prior to boarding and I will hail you when that time comes."

Byron had never seen such a sight as the ship moored to the quay. Floating before him was a huge man-of-war battleship, the HMS Vanguard. Protruding from the deck were three tall masts reaching to the heavens, and on the deck a menacing row of cannon and a second row below them. She was an awesome beauty to behold. Byron thought perhaps the ship could hold the entire population of Shillingstone. Indeed it could, as it carried a complement of over seven hundred men and officers. HMS Vanguard was registered as a second-rate ship of the line with years of ocean having passed under her keel. With her lines secured to the dock sailors and workmen rushed to load mounds of goods into the bowels of the ship. Sufficient provisions were stowed on board for the crew, including adequate beer and rum for the long trip to Cape Colony, a British port in Africa, and then on to India.

In a short time the officer hailed the recruits and they shuffled aboard to their assigned quarter's two levels below the main deck. What Byron saw below was not commensurate with the beauty of the ship's exterior. He had never seen such a dark, damp, confined space. Other than the captain and officers, all the ship's crew were on the same deck. Each was provided with a hammock and a small chest for personal effects. This would be Byron's home until he reached Calcutta.

When the last officer was piped aboard, lines were cast off and HMS Vanguard was towed to the main channel. Under partial sail she crossed the bar and headed for the open sea and a journey of eleven thousand five hundred miles around the Cape of Good Hope to India. Depending on sailing conditions, the journey would take from five to six months.

"All hands on deck!" came an order from the First Lieutenant, which had been prepared by Captain Josiah

Wentworth. All rules and regulations were read and strict discipline would be enforced, with punishment as necessary.

While the crew knew what this meant, Byron didn't. The Lieutenant continued, "The captain wants all to know HMS Vanguard is a sturdy ship with a good crew, and he prays God will give us good weather and fair sailing." In addition, the crew was told that there were a total of seven hundred and seventy-three souls on board, comprised of officers, crew, gunners and Bengal Artillery recruits. They were also informed that the HMS Vanguard was a Man-of-War and carried seventy-eight cannon.

As they sailed down the coast of France and Spain they were blessed with fair winds and following seas. The ship's crew established a daily rhythm of meal preparation, ship maintenance, adjusting sails, and swabbing decks with vinegar water. Most jack-tars, as English sailors were called, were experienced sea salts of the Royal Navy. In addition there were some rancorous conscripts and a few who had been gang pressed. With men of such ilk, it was only a matter of time before conflict would erupt.

In the meantime recruits were establishing their own pecking order. Since Byron was tall and muscular, he was selected as spokesman for the recruits. Their mission to fight with the Bengal Horse Artillery developed a bond of friendship and cooperation among them. Challenges were yet to come.

For the first month rolling seas were tolerable, even for a landlubber like Byron. During this time He had set up a schedule for when five recruits could go up to the main deck. It was an opportunity to get some exercise and experience the rising sun over the wide open horizon or the canopy of stars at night. In an environment of uncertainty there was an underlying excitement in this new venture.

They had been sailing through the trade belt with fresh winds and bright sunshine toward the meridian of the Cape of Good Hope A pod of porpoises was seen frisking and gamboling in the waves, playing leap-frog as they tumbled around the ship's bow. On several occasions a school of flying fish would swim alongside the ship and fly in the air. Byron and his comrades had never seen the like.

Several weeks before the Cape, the HMS Vanguard found herself in a heavy rising sea accompanied by strong winds. The sea and wind were turning foul and the captain shouted "All hands on deck and furl the main sail." Sailors scampered up the rigging like a troop of circus monkeys. The sails were quickly secured when a command came to "Secure storm sails." In quick succession orders were to make fast all casks and items on deck. Then all hands were ordered below to secure the hatches.

The wind roared, sails flapped noisily, and seas churned with eighteen-foot swells. Waves smashed over the bow, washing over the decks and cascading cold salt water below. Byron had never experienced this before and he was not sure what would happen. At home he had plowed the earth, but now he was in a ship plowing through a turbulent ocean. It was pitch dark with no lanterns or fires allowed for light. Creaking timbers and the smell of the salty seas were all new to him. Byron was learning that the transition from landlubber to seafarer would be a painful process. He was too tall to stand erect below deck and every movement required him to bend over or bang his head on a beam, which occurred frequently. In rolling seas, he sat on the wet floor with one arm around a ship's beam and the other holding fast to a bucket. Along with other recruits he was seasick and heaving generously into a pail and felt like his insides were swishing around at the bottom. A few men moaned and said they wanted to die.

Water was everywhere. Sea water poured down from decks above and some along the seams of the ships siding. Manual bilge pumps had to be manned twenty-four hours a day during the storm. It was a difficult and daunting task. Byron and his comrades were asked to take their turn and with difficulty did. For two days every living being below deck was sloshed around in complete darkness without water to drink or sleep to be attained. Finally, after what seemed like forever, the storm slowly abated. All aboard hoped they would survive to reach India. Byron again wondered if he had made the right decision.

"LAND HO!" drifted down from the crow's nest. After more than two months at sea they were approaching Cape Colony, Africa. Before rounding the Cape of Good Hope, Captain Wentworth decided to lay up for fresh provisions and letters from England. Only several handpicked crew members were allowed on shore to assist with loading supplies. For two days the ship's crew scurried onboard to make necessary repairs, paint and tar necessary rigging. The captain insisted the ship be maintained in pristine condition.

However, in the dead of night, one sailor who had been gang pressed escaped the ship, hoping to find passage back to England. Like his fellow seamen, he knew nothing about Africa. When he headed inland he realized he was in wild animal country. He had a choice of being eaten by a lion or returning to the ship to be whipped with the cat-o-nine tails. When he returned, he was immediately shackled and thrown into the brig, where he would be given bread and water until his punishment would be meted at sea.

A day prior to departing Cape Colony, the crew was informed that they could write letters home to be put on the next ship sailing for England. Byron wrote:

> Sarah: I arrived safely at a place called Cape Colony at the end of Africa. We are half way to India and I will write when I arrive. I think of you often. I miss you and love you. Byron.

A week back at sea, the captain decided on punishment for the sailor who had deserted the ship. He was to receive twenty-five lashes with the cat-o-nine tails. All hands were ordered on deck to witness his punishment. The prisoner was secured to a post, his clothes removed to the waist and the ship's mate read his sentence of twenty-five lashes. Byron had never heard of such cruel punishment and stood transfixed. The chief boatswain's mate was handed the whip and ordered by the captain, "Do your duty fully. If you slack you shall take his place."

One sailor counted the lashes, "One, two, three, four," and finally, "Twenty-five." Still barely conscious, the prisoner moaned, as his entire back was torn and bleeding. After being untied he was helped to his hammock and required to report for duty the next morning. Byron was aghast at the severity of such punishment.

Below deck there was an argument over the lashing. An old sea salt felt it was fair and respectful for the crew. A large gang-pressed sailor disagreed. He felt the captain was weak and lenient with just twenty-five lashes. A fight ensued and the bully nearly beat the old sailor to death before an officer on duty jumped into the melee and knocked the tyrant unconscious with a belaying pin. Then he was carried to the brig.

When he was informed about the disruption, Captain Josiah Wentworth acted quickly. All hands were ordered on deck to witness another use of the cat-o-nine tails. The conscript who caused the fight was tied to a post and his punishment read aloud: "One hundred lashes." A murmur of agreement was heard among the crew. When his punishment was concluded, no more problems occurred for the remainder of the voyage. Byron still felt unsettled, again having seen the cruel use of the cat-o-nine tails. Back home people were not treated like that.

Aboard the HMS Vanguard Byron and his fellow recruits knew nothing about gunnery. Now he was aboard a British "Man-O-War" bristling with 78 cannon. Was there an opportunity for him and his fellow recruits to learn how to fire a cannon? Representing the recruits, Byron asked the chief gunnery officer if he would be willing to show them the use of the ship's cannon. Without question the man would be pleased to do so, subject to approval from Captain Wentworth. Approval was granted.

Gunnery Officer Clark had been on numerous ships and had fired cannon in battles at sea and to breach the walls of a fort. A better instructor was not to be found aboard HMS Vanguard. In the following days he demonstrated loading, firing, washing, reloading and lighting a fuse to set off the huge gun. He explained that the cast iron ball weighed thirty pounds and created incredible damage. Each cannon required five or more gunners each with a specific assignment to clean the barrel, to load the gunpowder, to insert ball, to jam in wadding, and to prime and fire. He emphasized that firing cannon on rolling seas was very dangerous.

Byron asked if it would be possible to fire a cannon to demonstrate every movement of gunners in preparation for a shot. The ship's captain agreed to a single shot of a thirty pounder in calm seas. None of the recruits were prepared for the incredible boom, concussion, smoke, and power when a cannon was fired. Several months later they would find this to be a common experience.

Apart from some unsettling weather, the remainder of the voyage was uneventful. In April of 1856 the good ship HMS Vanguard sailed into the Bay of Bengal and, at high tide, sailed 160 miles up the Hooghly River to Calcutta. As the ship docked in Calcutta harbor, Byron saw a world he never knew existed. Here was an old city with elephants and camels walking the streets, men in peculiar clothing, odd-shaped buildings, strange sounds and pervasive smells which he had never experienced. He was in India.

RED MEN

Byron and his fellow recruits knew little about Calcutta or Camp Dum Dum, the military garrison named after a nearby village of the same name. All thirty-seven young men were loaded onto open wagons and transported to their camp which looked old and was old. Only a Union Jack on the camp's flagpole appeared new. Once assembled, they were welcomed by the commander's aide-de-camp. He explained, "The British have had a presence on the grounds of Camp Dum Dum for over two centuries. All this time it has been administered by the British East India Company as an artillery base manufacturing cannon and ammunition. Since the turn of the century it has been home for the Bengal Horse Artillery. The commander and I welcome you as you train to become part of the fraternity of Red Men."

The moniker Red Men stemmed from the long red horsehair mane which hung from the top of their brass-mounted Roman style helmets. When horses galloped at full speed, the red mane flew in the air, letting the enemy identify they soon would encounter the crack Bengal Horse Artillery.

Before the start of a demanding training program they were given two days to settle into their barracks, put their uniforms in order, receive and write letters home.

Byron had told Sarah to send her letters to Camp Aldershot and from there they would be forwarded to his location. Knowing he would be sailing from Portsmouth, she wrote a letter hoping it would reach him before he left. She was not sure if he would ever receive it.

My dear Byron: It is hard to believe you are not here. I miss you already. Both my men are gone, my father most of the time and you my love, for seven years. I feel alone. I love you more than ever. I am praying for you and for your safe return. At night I dream we are married and living on a small farm next to your father's. It is such a happy thought. Daylight brings me back to reality. Write when you are able and let me know that you are safe. All my love, every day. Sarah.

Sarah, it was a real surprise when I received your letter. It must have been on the same ship on which I sailed. I arrived safely in this land of camels, elephants and strange looking people. Sailing here took five months of smooth sailing and a few days of rough seas. Right now

I am in an old military camp and about to start my artillery training. While sailing here I thought about you many, many times. I am lonely not seeing you or being with you. I love you and miss you. All my love, Byron

He could not bring himself to admit that he might have made a mistake by not waiting in Shillingstone.

After several days, recruits assembled in a large room to learn about the Bengal Horse Artillery, its history, its objectives in battle, and its fire power. The artillery consisted of six, nine, and twelve pound smooth bore cannon with a range of three hundred to twelve hundred yards. At three hundred yards its shot was as level as the horizon, which was close enough to enable a gunner to see the color of his enemy's eyes.

Each cannon was secured atop a caisson pulled by a team of six horses, with three gunners mounted on each horse on the right. The gunner on the front right horse directed the unit into battle. The corps was most effective when they charged to the front of a battle. At full gallop, an order of "Halt, action front" meant stop, turn one hundred-eighty degrees, load and be ready to fire in less than a minute. An experienced team could fire a shot every thirty seconds, either a cannonball, canister, or grapeshot. A benefit of an artillery corps of this nature was its speed and flexibility in battle.

A dozen recruits failed basic training and were given the choice of joining the regular Bengal Army or being transported back to England. Having suffered exhausting heat and humidity for six months all twelve chose England's cool damp temperatures. Byron completed his training with honors and was given his uniform which included the iconic brass-mounted Roman style helmet with a long red mane hanging from the top. He was sworn into the *corps d'elite* of the Bengal Horse Artillery.

Three months after arriving in Calcutta, Byron was surprised to receive a bundle of letters from Sarah. He spread them out on his bunk and arranged them by date, and slowly read each one. He read them over several times. She loved him and missed him greatly. Byron was both happy and sad, happy to get her letters and sad they were so far apart. Knowing she loved him made it a little easier. She had yet to receive any of his letters. Mail took a long time to travel to and from home.

When training was completed each recruit was assigned to an existing unit of the Bengal Horse Artillery. Byron became part of a fully-equipped and experienced squad of six artillery units, each having a caisson with six horses. Most soldiers in the group were from England, Ireland or Scotland. His commander was Captain Alexander McGregor, a Scotsman, who left no doubt who was in charge. A veteran of five years with the Artillery, he had served honorably in battles across India. He expected the best from every man under his command. Over the next week he ordered his squads to check their equipment, their ammunition supply, and the health of their horses. There were rumors of unrest within the Bengal army and Captain McGregor wanted his men to be prepared to move quickly.

The East India Company administered the country by the authority of a charter given in 1600 from the Crown which gave them the exclusive rights to trade in India. By 1855 the Company had reached the zenith of its success, having subjugated the entire subcontinent of India. Its standing army of two hundred and sixty thousand was larger than the regular British army. A majority of the militia were native Hindus, Muslims and Sikhs, commonly called sepoys. Unfortunately for decades they had been mistreated, discriminated against in pay, and in promotions and in respect. Christian missionaries exacerbated their resentment by trying to make converts and change their centuries-old caste system. A seething cauldron of rage needed only a spark to create a mutiny within the Bengal army. It came in an uncommon and unforeseen manner.

Gunpowder charge for the new British Army Enfield rifles came wrapped in a paper cartridge covered with animal fat. Sepoys were required to bite off the end of the cartridge. They refused to put the cartridges in their mouth as consuming beef or pork fat would violate a major tenant of their religion. Regrettably English officers ignored their religious beliefs and demanded they follow orders. Many refused.

What began as a resistance exploded into a mutiny by tens of thousands of Hindus, Muslims and Sikhs. Anyone English became a target of their wrath. Missionary families, including men, women, children and infants were brutally murdered. Those natives not supporting the mutiny were also massacred by the thousands. Gathering strength in numbers, thirty thousand sepoy mutineers successfully captured the Fortress Delhi, challenging the authority of the British East India Company to rule India. Directors of the company were slow to comprehend the ferocity and depth of the mutiny. When they finally realized they could lose all of India, they called up all the military resources of the Company to defeat the murderous rampaging mutineers.

The first battle began in the city of Patna, midway between Calcutta and Fort Delhi. It was also important as it produced eighty percent of the opium that was shipped to China. The East India Company could ill afford to lose this enormous source of income as the battle to keep India would come at an enormous financial cost.

A military force of ten thousand was quickly assembled with orders to retake the city that had been overtaken by seven thousand mutineers. Following the ancient Grand Trunk highway, the Bengal Horse Artillery were the first to arrive outside Patna. They would not be able to defeat the enemy, but would give them a taste of what was coming. With thirty units under his command, Captain McGregor ordered twenty units to fire on the center with five other units on each flank. When the first ray of sun rose above the horizon they were to attack. This would be Byron's first experience in battle. His unit was ordered to fire and charge at the center defensive line of the enemy.

Prior to sunrise the company's horses began snorting and stamping the ground as if they sensed something was about to happen. Gunners rapidly harnessed their horses to their respective caissons. When the sun breached the horizon, all hell broke loose. Each Artillery unit faced heavy incoming cannon fire. They advanced at a full gallop and were swiftly below enemy cannonballs that flew over them like black lumps of coal. While charging the enemy, something clipped Byron's right shoulder, ripping his uniform. When he looked back he saw a headless horseman, decapitated by a cannon ball, but still atop his horse. At six hundred yards, the command came: "Halt action front." In seconds, a blizzard of cannon shot from the Bengal Horse Artillery took some fight out of the enemy. After a second volley of grapeshot the mutineer's guns fell silent and Captain McGregor's forces returned to their temporary camp, a safe distance from Patna.

Of the two-hundred and ten gunners, twelve men had been killed and twenty-one wounded. A similar number of horses had been killed or injured. Exhausted, Byron returned to camp having experienced the acrid smell, sound and carnage of battle. He had been alarmed at the ferocity of the exchange of artillery fire. He felt fortunate to have survived his first battle and was sad for those who died and his comrades who were wounded.

With the arrival of additional forces from Calcutta, the equation of battle changed. Ten thousand English would now face an estimated force of seven thousand mutineers. General Sir James Belford was commander of the army and had a reputation for successful campaigns. In a matter of two days his force was rested, armed and ready for battle. Taking into account the terrain and a motivation for revenge, he believed it would be a single battle and he would be victorious.

General Belford chose a classic battle plan where he would attack the enemy's center with an overpowering force. Simultaneous attacks would be made on both enemy flanks. Once the center broke, fierce fighting would be hand to hand. The battle would be brutal with no quarter given or received as Sikh rebels had a reputation of fighting to the last man.

Before the light of day fifty army artillery thirty- pound cannon let loose a continuous barrage of fire against the defensive line of the mutineers and continued for five hours. Midmorning Balford ordered the Bengal Horse Artillery to attack the center of their defense. Byron and his units attacked, followed by thousands of loyal foot soldiers of the Bengal Army.

Byron's caisson closed on the enemy and did a 'halt, action, front.' At close range his unit proceeded to pound the mutineer's line. Although damaged from the previous cannon fire, the mutineers still had a lot of fight left. With the support of the infantry and the close range of the Bengal Horse artillery, the battle was over by late afternoon. General Belford's prediction had come true.

There was considerable loss of life on both sides of the battle. No prisoners were taken. Byron's caisson lost two men and four horses. He was fortunate to survive intact, but was exhausted. Before returning to camp Byron surveyed the field of battle and was astounded at the carnage and loss of life of the enemy. General Belford's forces suffered fewer loses but the implications of those losses would be felt by their comrades, and families back home.

A month later the Bengal Horse Artillery were ordered back to their base in Calcutta. Most were pleased to be back and looked forward to letters from home. Byron was no exception. After the hell he had experienced in Patna, he yearned for the tranquility of Shillingstone and longed to hear from Sarah. He was pleased when he received a bundle of her letters.

> *My dearest Byron: I pray every day that you are safe and will stay safe. My love becomes stronger every day and I miss you more than ever. I had doubts about getting married right away. I now believe that was a mistake I would not make again even though my family situation has not changed. I would love to be your wife. Much love, Sarah*

Sara's other letters were much the same as the first, telling what was happening at home. Byron was in a quandary over what he could say about his first battle. How could he tell her about the hell he went through and then switch to expressions of love?

> Sarah: Every day I look forward to receiving your letters and I read them thoroughly. It was wonderful to hear that you now agree to get married when I return. It is my fondest wish. I often think about the wonderful times we had taking the trap to the River Stour. I would like to visit many of the places we went when I return to Shillingstone. I have come to enjoy my military experience and many of my comrades. I love you and am committed to our decision to be man and wife. Love Byron.

Back in the Calcutta garrison Byron and his fellow artillery men recuperated and resumed their daily routines. Few talked about what they had just experienced. Byron had difficulty contrasting the peaceful life he experienced growing up at home with the death and suffering of battle.

Fortress Delhi had been captured by thirty thousand sepoys who had declared it to be the new capital for all of

India. Encamped five miles to the south, twelve thousand British soldiers fought to hold their positions until help could arrive to retake the fortress. They were in a precarious position and were regularly attacked from the fort.

In Calcutta an enormous British build-up began for a final battle hundreds of miles north in Delhi. A caravan stretched out over forty miles from Calcutta. More than twenty thousand soldiers were on the march with two thousand mounted cavalry, followed by twenty elephants, each pulling a large siege cannon. Eight sleds of ammunition were pulled by twenty team bullocks. In addition, the quartermaster loaded over a hundred wagons with provisions of food for the soldiers, and feed for the livestock. It was estimated that it would take six or more months to reach Fortress Delhi. The Grand Trunk highway from Calcutta to Delhi had never experienced such abuse as this massive military convoy moved north to Fortress Delhi.

An early spring brought unusual heat to the Bengal region. At midday temperatures often soared to one hundred and twenty degrees. Both soldiers and animals suffered from the excessive heat. General Belford gave the order to travel at night and rest during the day. Travel was hot, grueling and slow.

A small contingent of Byron's Bengal Horse Artillery arrived before the main column and joined the battle outside Fortress Delhi, giving support to the beleaguered encampment. No sooner had the Bengal Horse Artillery arrived when they were attacked by nearly a thousand mutineers who charged out from the fort. Byron and ten other units went into "action front" and prepared to fire at the charging enemy who had closed to within five hundred yards. Byron loaded the muzzle of his cannon with grape shot and fired, killing a plethora of mutineers, but they kept coming. Byron was now face on with three enemy sepoys. He shot two with his double barrel carbine giving him seconds to load his cannon with more grape shot. As Byron rammed the shot down the barrel, an enraged mutineer with menacing eyes charged Byron with a cutlass raised above his head shouting "Death...death!" Byron quickly stepped aside and simultaneously drew a sword from his scabbard. When the mutineer turned around to charge again Byron drove him through with his sword. His menacing eyes went blank and his mouth was open but silent, his knees buckled as he dropped dead at Byron's feet. After a second grape shot the enemy retreated.

Exhausted, Byron leaned against the wheel of his caisson and viewed the butchery of battle that surrounded him. The dead bodies of three rebels lay at his feet. Mangled bodies of soldiers and mutineers lay mixed in a field of discarded material of war. Cannons were silent and were replaced by the cries of wounded men and the grunting horses about to be destroyed. Acrid smoke that covered the field of battle made it difficult to breath. He was fortunate to be alive.

In recognition of his courage during the battle Byron was promoted to second lieutenant. It was rare to appoint an officer who was not of the gentleman class, but battle deaths and the wounded had greatly reduced the number of commissioned officers. Byron was recognized for his military acumen and leadership, which led the army command to make this unusual decision.

During a lull in fighting Byron had time to think about the battle he had just survived. He had never killed a man with a sword, however it was kill or be killed. The face to face death of that mutineer would never escape his memory.

When the entire military force arrived outside Fortress Delhi they promptly assembled their siege cannon and mercilessly pounded the fort. After two months of constant cannon fire the walls began to crumble. General Belford prepared his soldiers to charge the fort when more than one gate was blown apart. Belford's force of twenty thousand faced thirty thousand of the enemy. This day would determine who won or lost India. Enraged by the memory of thousands of English who were massacred, the infantry rushed through multiple gates and charged into the sepoys. It was fierce hand-to-hand combat. It was not until late afternoon that the General rushed in his reserves and the fighting turned in his favor. His soldiers ultimately defeated the mutineers and the fort fell to the British.

The remaining rebels surrendered and justice was swift. Hundreds of mutineers who had participated in murdering civilians and killed loyal native soldiers were summarily dispatched by firing squad, hanged, or put to the cannon. The rebellion that began in 1857 was over by August of 1858.

Finally the East India Company again controlled the subcontinent of India, but in the process paid an enormous price in manpower and a staggering financial cost. They had won the war and lost their company. With the impending bankruptcy the English Parliament dissolved the East India Company and the subcontinent of India now became a colony of the Crown. Queen Victoria was declared Empress of India and India became the Jewel in the Crown of the British Empire.

Several months passed before the Bengal Horse Artillery members made their way back to their home base in Dum Dum. They had lost fifty men in Delhi, three of whom were Byron's close friends. Though the Bengal Army emerged victorious, the death of fellow soldiers left no room for celebration by Byron or any of his comrades. On arriving at the Dum Dum garrison Byron hoped Sarah's letters would lift his spirits and transport his mind to the beauty and tranquility of Shillingstone.

DOUBT AND DECISION

Sarah went to the post office so many times it felt like her second home. This was the place she could connect with the love of her life, through his letters. Incoming mail arrived at the post office at 6:00 a.m. and 1:15 p.m. daily, except weekends. Her mother's needs and Christopher's health made it difficult to get there early, but it was a rare day she missed the afternoon mail.

Henry Chamberlin had been Shillingstone's postmaster for as long as she could remember. He was a kindly old gentleman with a white beard, a wrinkled face and wire rimmed glasses hanging on the end of his nose. Everyone knew the postmaster, and he knew everyone. Since Byron left to join the army, he had come to know Sarah very well. In a way he adopted her as one of his grandchildren. "Young lady, it's good to see you again," was his usual greeting when Sarah showed up at his postal window.

"Well, I suppose it is the same today as it was yesterday." This was Sarah's usual response when a letter from Byron had not arrived.

"It seems to be that when more than a month has passed, a letter or so shows up a month later. It takes a long time for a letter to arrive here all the way from India." The postmaster continued, "Sergeant Wilson had the same problem years ago when he wrote to his family, as he served his country in India. I had a special slot for him and now one for you when a letter arrives."

"Thank you Mr. Chamberlin, see you tomorrow."

Sarah was disappointed but not surprised. At least she had some letters at home that she could read over again. The bakery was near the post office so she decided to stop by for bread. As a child she came with her mother early in the morning when the bread was fresh from the oven. However, caring for her mother and Christopher made it impossible. She hoped there was some bread left.

When she entered the store she was greeted with, "Hello, just come from the post office?" It was the baker's wife who greeted her

"Yes, and the same news, no letter."

"Sorry to hear that. What can I get for you?"

"Since none of us are big eaters the usual white loaf will do."

"There's a couple left. Which one do you want?"

"The last one on the right will be fine." Sarah took the loaf and put it in a cloth bag that she had brought with her.

"Have you heard from your father about the railroad coming?"

"No. He's home so seldom I've heard very little. I think he said they were going to work on a route from Blandford

Forum to here, nothing more. When he is home he doesn't like to talk about his work." Sarah paid for the bread and said, "Thank you."

When Sarah arrived at home her mother was still having her afternoon nap. Christopher was sitting on a bench at the kitchen table reading from a book. He was always happy to see her back home.

Caring for her mother was difficult as Mildred was unpredictable. For short periods of time she seemed normal and at other times she was in a world of her own. When anxious, she sipped a mixture of water and laudanum to calm herself down. Sarah was disturbed that her mother refused to have any relationship with Christopher. She believed her mother blamed his birth for her present condition. Other than a letter from Byron, Christopher was the only one that brought her any joy.

Christopher was now six years old and Sarah had developed a special bond with him. His body was weak, but his mind was strong. She taught him songs and rhymes she had learned from her mother. By now he was also able to read and write. From infancy she was the one that rocked him in a rocking chair and patted his back when breathing was difficult. Sarah chose not to think about what might happen to him in the future.

The next day Sarah was back at the post office. "Well it's good to see you this afternoon young lady." The post man greeted her.

"I guess there's no letter for me?"

"No there isn't, not today. But there is some good new going around. You remember the Portland family who gave land for a village school."

"I do, that was the year Byron asked me to marry him."

"It was. I hear they'll start building the school early this year. I hope they teach good penmanship so I can read anything that comes to the post office that, is if I'm still here."

"Mr. Chamberlin, you will live forever."

"Hush now, you scoot along and I will see you tomorrow."

It was always nice to see the post master, but most of the time she left disappointed a letter had not come from Byron. Back in her cottage Sarah would sit in front of the fireplace and dream about the day when she and Byron would be married. This image and his letters kept her alive.

Byron was resting on his bed reading Sarah's letters when he came to the realization that he would be returning home a different man. In the past months he had faced the horrors of war with its life and death consequences. He decided that he would never be able to share these experiences with Sarah.

Then he turned his thoughts to their love and the future they would share when he returned.

Byron now faced a decision that would change the direction of his life as well as the life of others. With the mutiny over and India now under the rule of the British Crown, the Bengal Horse Artillery was to be amalgamated with the Royal Army Artillery. In 1861 Byron was given the choice of transferring to the British Royal Artillery in India or returning to Aldershot. He decided to return and was granted passage back to England. This time he would enter the camp a Second Lieutenant rather than a hunble recruit. His return would be a surprise for Sarah as there was not sufficient time to get a letter to her.

A new steamship, the HMS Warrior, would shortly be sailing from Calcutta to Portsmouth with an estimated sailing time of 45 days, including a stop for coal in Cape Colony. This was a new steel-hulled ship that had been at sea only since 1860. She was fast and powerful and was served by a complement of 700 seamen and officers of the Royal Navy.

On board Byron was amazed at the accommodations for the ship's crew. Every jack-tar had a uniform, a table for meals and a clean hammock hanging above the cannon deck. However, difficult and dangerous work was still a sailor's bane. With an option of steam or sail, HMS Warrior parted the waves with ease.

As his ship plowed through the sea, Byron wondered about Sarah. What would she look like? Was her situation at home better? Did she still want to get married? Answers would have to wait. Finally, in early summer of 1861, Byron arrived in Portsmouth. From there he sent a telegram telling Sarah that he would see her in three days. Sarah was surprised and nervous by the telegram. "What was he going to say? Had he changed? It has been months since I got a letter from him. What am I going to say?"

When Byron's coach entered Blandford Road, nothing appeared to have changed. To the surprise of postmaster Chamberlin, Byron dropped his luggage off in his care. From behind his window Mr. Chamberlin shouted, "Son, it's good to see you and welcome home." Byron forgot that now everyone would know he was back home. Then he began the trek to Sarah's cottage on Poplar Hill. The cottage looked the same as he remembered it.

Sarah heard a rustle outside her door and opened it to find Byron standing in front of her. She threw her arms about him, almost causing him to fall. No better display of joy could be found. For what seemed like a long time, no words were spoken. Sarah cried out, "I love you, I love you!"

Bryon responded, "Those are words I have been waiting to hear."

Sarah took him by the hand and dragged him into the cottage. When he was last there Sarah's brother was only four and Byron was not sure Christopher would remember him. So he introduced himself and reached down and shook his hand. Christopher responded with a broad smile and handshake. Sarah's mother was sleeping and Edward was working in Shrewsbury. Sitting in front of the fireplace with a fresh cup of tea, they chatted about the years they had been apart, much of it a repeat of their letters with a sprinkle of additional news. The topic of marriage never came up. Neither knew what to say. After several hours, Byron excused himself and went to his father's farm with the promise to return.

Howard was puttering around his front yard when he saw a man approaching whom he didn't recognize. As he came closer he realized it was his son, Byron. He had left home a young man, and now a mature man had returned. With a firm handshake his father welcomed him home. Moisture in Howard's eyes was not sufficient to create a tear but had the same effect. For the remainder of the afternoon and into the evening, father and son talked about the years he had been away. They walked about the farm, then sat outside and shared memories. Howard wanted to know about his time in India. But Byron wanted to know about the farm, what was he planting, how was the harvest? Does he have the same animals? Finally, they spoke about being at home again. Howard was more than pleased that he had come home safely.

Over the next several weeks Byron and Sarah spent as much time together as possible. They sat on the banks of the Stour River, took rides in the country and shared meals in Sarah's cottage. All the time Sarah was wondering if Byron had the same emotional feeling toward her as before he left. She believed her love was just the same as before. His letters said he still loved her and wanted to get married. Now that he was home she wondered if his love was the same as in his letters.

On one occasion they were walking along the banks of the Stour River enjoying the sights and sounds when Byron stopped and turned directly to Sarah. He didn't say anything for a few moments, he just looked at her. Sarah wondered, "What is he going to say?"

Then Byron spoke, "Sarah I cannot count the many times I have thought of you, missed you, and loved you. I would lie on my bed and read your letters over and over again. In my mind I visualized you just as I see you now. I love you now just as much as I have ever loved you. When I return I look forward to our getting married." They kissed tenderly.

If Sarah had any doubts about how Byron felt about her, they dissipated. What did not disappear was the wait for when he would returned home.

One person Byron wanted to see was Sergeant Wilson. There was a good chance the old fellow would be at the Old Ox Inn, and indeed, there he was in his usual chair with his usual pint in hand. At first the sergeant did not recognize Byron, but after a moment Wilson was ecstatic. Aware that Byron was now a Second Lieutenant, he stood and was about to salute, when Byron said, "Not necessary sergeant, I'm not on duty. I'll get a pint and we can visit." Now both shared stories of battle and heroism while in India with the Bengal Horse Artillery. Sergeant Wilson was saddened to learn about the amalgamation of his old unit with the British Army

Artillery, and he was glad he had retired. It was a grand afternoon of shared memories between two comrades.

All too soon, Byron's leave came to an end. With two years left on his seven year military commitment he would soon learn what awaited him when he returned to Camp Aldershot. He bade a fond farewell to Sarah and assured her he would write often.

ALDERSHOT II

After his thirty day leave Byron arrived at a different Camp Aldershot. Since he had entered in 1855, more buildings had been erected, streets had been finished, lawns were manicured and trees were neatly trimmed. What was once temporary was now permanent. An aura of military pride was clearly evident, and it made him proud to be part of the British Army.

His first responsibility was to report for duty at the base headquarters. The Base Commander General Sir John Pennefather was a quintessential military commander who stood rigidly erect, dressed impeccably in his uniform, and sported a waxed gray mustache that extended beyond his cheeks. He had been informed that Byron would report and looked forward to meeting him as they both had fought in India.

After a military salute, Second Lieutenant Fletcher was ordered to stand easy. Commander Pennefather welcomed him to Camp Aldershot and informed him they had several things in common. Both had clergy in their family; the General's father was a vicar, as was Byron's grandfather. Pennefather had begun his military career in the 7th Dragoon Guards, similar to what lay ahead for Byron. Most important for the general was the fact that they had both fought in India. Without attention to time, they talked extensively about their battle experiences.

"I believe, Lieutenant, that your assignment to India was more recent than mine."

"Yes sir, it was during the Indian rebellion which was recently won after some hard-fought battles. I was fortunate enough survive several close encounters."

"My military experience in India occurred some fifteen or more years earlier. It was a heady time when the Bengal Army was the sole military authority in most of India. No one thought, including myself, that there would ever be a mutiny within the Bengal soldiers. A large divide had existed between the English and the native soldiers. When you fought your battles I was back in England and eventually assigned here to Aldershot. Thank you for cleaning up our mess."

"Sir, I have heard several accounts of your military excursions in India which set the standard for our actions which followed. I look forward to being under your command while here in Camp Aldershot."

"Thank you for our short repartee, perhaps we can continue it later. Lieutenant, you are dismissed."

The commander had been impressed with the Second Lieutenant and would follow his career with interest.

Byron was assigned to the First Dragoon Light Horse Cavalry and, due to his military record in India, was promoted to full lieutenant. He was among young officers being oriented to the regiment who had a proud and storied history of successful battles in many parts of the world. Byron was one of fifty young men designated to become a cavalry officer. Since he was the only one with mounted experience, he was elected their officer-in-command.

Training was intensive and exhausting. His unit was being trained to do reconnaissance, command communication, and to fight as opportunity arose. Light Calvary units seldom made a frontal charge unless supported by the infantry. Every mounted officer was equipped with a sword and a short barrel carbine and was expected to be proficient in their use.

Horse and rider learned to overcome their natural instincts. Horses naturally balk at the smell of blood, the boom of cannon, and confined spaces, but they could be trained to overcome these challenges. Only time and practice would allow a cavalry officer to ride his mount at full speed and use his sword, pistol or carbine with lethal effect. With sore muscles, bumps, bruises and an occasional broken bone, all fifty recruits became qualified cavalrymen.

In the summer of 1861, General Pennefather received an urgent message from the Court of Queen Victoria. He was ordered to select twenty five of his best cavalry officers for an assignment in Shanghai, China. While the contingent would not be large, the Crown wanted a British military presence in the European community in Shanghai. When they arrived they would be under the command of the storied General Charles "Chinese" Gordon.

Again, on the basis of his experience Byron was appointed officer-in-command of this cavalry unit. Within two weeks all were aboard the sail/steam ship HMS Black Prince and were bound for the port of Shanghai.

During the voyage Byron and his comrades were apprised of their assignment. Few, if anyone, knew anything about China. A liaison officer explained the situation as best he could. He told them that Hong Xiugan, a religious zealot in an adulterated interpretation of Christianity, believed he was the brother of Jesus and established a religion followed by millions of disenfranchised Chinese. He was charismatic and successful in building an enormous army.

Their objective was to overthrow the Buddhist Manchu Emperor and make a "Heavenly Kingdom of Peace" in all of China. Eventually a war, known as the Taiping Rebellion, was fought between the two groups of differing religions. England, as well as France, had no interest in this civil war until a threat came to the doorstep of the European trading community in Shanghai.

In 1861, the army of the "Heavenly Kingdom of Peace" attacked Shanghai's sizable European community. In response, the British Army in China, made up of three thousand European soldiers known as the "Ever Victorious Army" prepared to defend their turf. This army was under the command of General Gordon, and was allied with the Manchu Emperor's army.

Shortly after Byron and his cavalry disembarked they were directed to the British garrison in Shanghai and introduced to their commander. General Gordon told them that they had four days to organize their cavalry units and be ready to move against the zealot's army. Their objective was to reconnoiter outside of Shanghai and assist the general in battle opposing the religious zealots. Saving the city of Shanghai would weaken the forces of the "Heavenly Kingdom of Peace."

Manchu generals uniformly made direct attacks against their enemy with little regard to casualties. In contrast, General Gordon's battles were carefully planned to prevent as many casualties as possible. Over the next three months their combined armies fought and defeated the enemy who had attacked Shanghai.

General Gordon was well informed and carefully planned his battles thus preventing many casualties. In contrast both Chinese armies appeared to simply throw their armies at each other creating enormous loss of life. Byron had never seen such carnage and death between warring armies.

During these battles five of his cavalry officers had been killed and two were seriously wounded. Byron was fortunate to escape with bruises when his horse was shot from under him.

During his assignment in China a letter came from Sarah that brought news that her brother had died.

> *My dearest Byron: I have*
> *some sad news to tell you. A*
> *short time ago Christopher's*

condition worsened and within a week of this crisis he died. He was only seven years old. He was the most important person in my life here in Shillingstone. I am devastated. My Aunt Edith tries to comfort me, but I know you are the only one who could help me through this crisis and you are not here. Neither is my father. I don't know what to do with my life. I love you, Sarah

Dearest Sarah: It is with sadness I just read your letter about Christopher's death. Here in India I am well acquainted with the grief that comes with death. It brings sadness to all that loved him. He was courageous in dealing with his sickness. You have my loving sympathy. It won't be long and I shall be home. Love, Byron.

Byron knew how much Sarah had loved Christopher and the special relationship they had as brother and sister. Over the next several weeks, he wondered if the sad loss of Sarah's brother might affect their future together. She made no reference about her mother. Would she be free to marry?

Although Byron's term of service was up in early 1862, the war in China continued. Byron had lost a few men in battle, and the "Ever Victorious Army" lost two hundred and thirty men out of three thousand. General Gordon's weapons and tactics accounted for the low number of losses. In contrast it was estimated that twenty million Chinese soldiers and civilians on both sides had died in the ongoing civil war.

Byron was ready to go home. China was far from Sarah and he had received few letters. Those that arrived were torn, wrinkled or dirty. Still, he savored every word and started to think about their life together. At home he would be removed from the horror of war.

DORSET CENTRAL RAILWAY

Since 1860 there had been indications that the Dorset Central Railway would be coming. All around the village railroad ties were piled up along the line's path where crews of Irish navvies had carved out a road bed for iron rails. Construction on the train depot had begun, confirming that the Dorset Central Railway was coming to Shillingstone.

By August of 1863 the Dorset Central Railway was complete. A major feature was an attractive train depot with a long raised platform and a two-story signal box for the stationmaster. When the final spike was driven into the ground, a general holiday was declared for the entire village. At the arrival of the first steam engine, the vicar and his wife invited everyone for tea in the rectory barn. A crowd quickly filled the tithe barn and overflowed to the surrounding grounds. It was a day many would remember.

With the arrival of the railway, change had come to Shillingstone. Social mobility, which had been limited, expanded. Young men and women were able to find potential partners beyond their village. No longer would households need to buy from the markets near their homes. Farmers and tradesmen could sell produce and merchandise to an extended population.

Most villagers had never traveled further than the nearest market town five miles away. Now they could visit Bournemouth by the sea, or go to London to see

Buckingham Palace. It was possible to discover a new world far beyond their village.

Sarah knew Byron's enlistment was up in 1863 and the Dorset Central train line would bring him home. She still felt guilty that she didn't do enough to help Christopher, and his loss was difficult for her to overcome. She hoped Byron's return would make her feel better.

While Byron was not able to be at Sarah's side during her bereavement, her Aunt Edith became a source of support. Earlier in the year she had moved to Shillingstone to be near her sister Mildred and her family. Her husband had died fifteen year earlier, leaving her with modest finances that allowed her to live independently in a prudent manner. She had rented a room from a widow whose cottage was close to where Sarah lived. With Sarah's father absent and her mother emotionally despondent, her aunt was the only person on whom Sarah could rely for help.

A telegram from Byron informed Sarah he would be arriving home by train in two days. With a burst of energy she tackled cleaning the cottage not once but twice. Any problems or challenges disappeared as the love of her life was coming home. Her world would be made right again. For a moment she looked out her old window with its wavy glass and tiny air bubbles and saw a glorious summer day. Her life would be better.

Early in the afternoon of the second day Sarah made her way to the new train depot where Byron was expected to arrive. All morning she had fussed with her hair, made sure her best dress was ready to wear and her face freshened. She made every effort to be as attractive as possible. The Dorset Central Railway had a reputation for late arrivals and today was no exception. Sarah was worried until she heard a train's whistle, a ringing brass bell, and the hiss of steam as the locomotive arrived and slowly came to a stop at the end of the platform. When passengers descended from the train Sarah was not sure which one was Byron, until he removed his cap displaying his bushy red hair. Her excitement erupted in the middle of a crowd of people as she dashed to Byron and, putting her arms around him, cried out, "I love you, I love you, I love you!" Byron was overjoyed to be home again.

After catching her breath, Sarah stood there admiring the wonderful man who had returned to her. They stood back just beaming at each other. Byron looked at Sarah and thought she was as beautiful as ever. They were together again after seven long years. Now they could think about their life together. Then Byron and Sarah made their way to her cottage.

On the way Byron turned to Sarah and said, "I know I wrote how bad I felt on the death of Christopher, but I don't think it was sufficient. I know how difficult it was for you and your mother and I will do all I can to help in your time of grief."

"Byron, your letter was very comforting, just as what you say right now." For the rest of the afternoon they caught up on each other's lives. As Sarah prepared supper they made small talk about how wonderful it was to be together again.

It began to feel like they had never been apart. When their meal was ready, Byron pulled out a bottle of wine from a small satchel. They celebrated his return and their future together. When he was about to leave, Sarah asked him to come by the next day. He agreed.

Before sunset Byron walked to his father's farm several miles away. Howard was sitting in front of his house smoking his pipe, enjoying the aroma of his favorite tobacco. When he saw his son he stood by the front door and greeted him with a father's embrace. Byron was safely home again! Howard listened to his son's many military adventures in India and China. It was a great evening and would be one of many in the days to come.

Word of Byron's arrival in Shillingstone spread quickly. No one from the village had ever traveled halfway around the world once, let alone twice. As he walked down Blandford Road he was frequently greeted by local shopkeepers. He made a point to stop at the post office to thank postmaster Chamberlin for handling their mail. Byron's comments were appreciated. As he passed the blacksmith's forge Klaus called out in his Austrian accent, "Velcome home!" Holding a red hot piece of steel with his tongs he continued banging on his anvil spacing his words between each pound of this hammer, "Vot.....do..... yer.....need?"

Byron replied, "Nothing, nothing at all." He noticed Klaus had a young apprentice so he shouted, "Teach the boy well."

With a smile and pound of his hammer Klaus responded, "I vill ….. I vill." Byron enjoyed his attention.

Over the next month Byron and Sarah spent a lot of time together, made possible by her aunt who now cared for her sister Mildred. They both felt good recalling the places they had visited, the memories they shared, as well as how much they loved and valued each other.

Their favorite place was on the banks of the Stour River. On one of their visits they were on a blanket silently enjoying the view. Sarah broke the silence when she commented, "You must have had many difficult experiences when you were away" Byron wondered when this subject might arise, but he had decided to leave out the horror of war and share other events.

"My first trauma was getting sea sick. One day the sea was very rough and many of us got so sick we felt like we would rather die. In India the temperature was extremely hot which required us to travel during the cool of the night. Language was a challenge in China. Few English spoke Chinese or Chinese English. There were other challenges, but these are still vivid in my memory." After a pause he continued, "Most of the time I thought about you. What kept me going was the hope that I would survive and know that I would return to be here with the one I love most in the world."

What Byron said took her breath away. She looked lovingly at him and with a tear sliding down her cheek she whispered, "I love you." No more was said. They lay on the blanket looking at a vivid blue sky, feeling a warm summer breeze float over them, and soaking in the passion of their love for each other.

Back at home Sarah asked Edith what she thought of Byron. Her aunt was impressed and said, "I thought he was confident, mature, attractive and considerate." She also understood he was well-traveled with experience about life far beyond the limits of Shillingstone. Sarah told Edith what she expected was coming and Edith smiled.

During their time together Byron had not forgotten that he wanted to marry Sarah. Did she still feel the same? He felt uncomfortable asking her directly. His view of women was still affected by his father's opinion that marriage to his mother was above his station as a simple farmer. Many times his father told him about his mother, and the sanctity of women. They were to be respected and given deference in life. Did this put Sarah on a higher level than him? Did this put him in the same place as his father? He wondered.

Sarah had worried a bit to see if military life had changed Byron. He was mature and in great physical condition, yet still possessed his wholesomeness. She recognized he was pleased that she was still the beautiful, pleasant, woman he remembered. This eased her worries.

All Byron wanted was to settle down, be married and raise a family. He hoped to rent a small farm with a cottage, space for some animals, and good soil for growing crops. He was excited thinking about the future of having a wife and a farm of their own.

Several days later Byron and Sarah again visited their favorite spot on the banks of the River Stour. It was a rare beautiful sunny summer day, and after an enjoyable trap ride, they spread out a blanket on the river's bank and quietly listened to the murmur of the river meandering around its curves with rippling water slinking over countless stones creating a calming whisper. In that serene setting Sarah sensed something was about to be said.

Byron looked at Sarah and began, "Sarah, during the seven years I have been away, I have experienced the horrors of war, the loss of comrades, sweltering heat and sickness, wondering if I would live another day. What gave me hope was knowing that I would return to the beautiful woman I love and we would become man and wife." After a short pause he continued, "Sarah, again I am asking you to marry me."

Sarah looked past him and said nothing. She ached to say yes, but couldn't. After taking a deep breath she whispered, "Byron, I love you and I want to be your wife." She took another breath, deep enough for her chest to expand and continued, "My emotions are raw from Christopher's death and the burden of my mother." With a quick breath and some hesitation she asked, "May I have two days to talk with my Aunt Edith and seek her advice?"

Byron was bewildered and speechless. After seven years of built-up emotions he had just bared his soul to Sarah and anticipated a simple yes. He was crushed. Suddenly everything was silent around them. When Byron didn't respond, Sarah began to cry. He didn't know what to do, think or say. Finally he suggested impatiently, "Perhaps you *should* talk to your aunt."

On the ride back to town their mood had changed from the excitement earlier in the day. On reaching Sarah's cottage, he gave Sarah a warm hug. They agreed to talk again soon and Bryon went home. For seven years he had made life and death decisions. Now he faced Sarah's equivocation. It would be frustrating and difficult, but again he agreed to wait a couple of days for her decision.

On the way back to the farm he stopped at the Old Ox Inn, hoping to find Sergeant Wilson. He was in his usual place. They were pleased to see each other and shared a pint. Byron was anxious to talk about what had just happened, but changed his mind and decided to relate his adventures in China. Sergeant Wilson was willing to listen. After several more pints, Byron finally ran out of stories and found his way home to bed.

After Byron left Sarah, she stood near the front door, her mind abuzz with conflicting thoughts with no clear direction. When she approached the front door she stopped. The cottage door was slightly ajar and she always latched it. When she entered she was shocked at what she saw. Her father was in a rocking chair with a bandaged foot resting on a box. She gasped, "What happened?"

Edward told her that he had tripped over a rail while surveying. He fell and injured his ankle which was purple and swollen. His supervisor told him to stay off his foot for a month. Her father told her, "At least I am fortunate you are at home and can take care of me,"

Sarah spent a restless night feeling trapped more than ever. What would she tell Byron? Exhausted, she finally fell asleep, having decided to visit her Aunt Edith in the morning. After fixing breakfast for her parents, Sarah walked the short distance to Edith's cottage. Tea and scones were on her table. With tears in her eyes Sarah spilled out all that had happened the previous day, including her father's accident. "I don't know what to do!"

Edith cautiously asked, "Do you want to marry him?"

Sarah replied confidently, "Yes."

"Then do it!" Edith emphatically exclaimed.

"How can I, with everything that's happened?" Sarah questioned hesitantly.

"Sarah, there are young women in the village who would say yes to Byron even before he would ask." Edith clearly explained.

Sarah asked, "Who would take care of my mother and father?"

"When your father's foot heals, it's his responsibility to care for his wife. In the meantime you'd have time to set a date for your wedding. If you don't marry the man you love now, you risk losing him."

Frustrated Sarah said, "I can't decide what to do!"

After finishing her tea, Sarah went home feeling worse than when she had come. She was looking for her aunt to solve her dilemma. Her advice was clear, but did not fix the conflict she was facing. If she married Byron, she would feel guilty about abandoning her parents. If she lost Byron to someone else, it would be her fault. The mantle of guilt was heavy and it felt unbearable. In trying to please everyone, she would please no one. She didn't know what to do.

Byron said he would pick her up the morning of the second day, and he did. They took a table where they had been before in a quiet corner at the Old Ox Inn. After toast and tea Byron came straight to the point, "Sarah, I thought of you every day for the seven years I have been away. I believed that when I returned we would be married. I love you and want you to be my wife forever. I want us to be married soon."

In response Sarah told him, "My father had an accident at work and will be at home for an indefinite amount of time. My mother continues to be a burden and the death of Christopher is still heavy on my mind. I don't know what to do!"

Byron was flummoxed. Waiting seven years had changed nothing. Would waiting any longer make a difference? He loved her but felt helpless. She loved him and felt the same. Her family problems had become his. Byron needed some perspective in sorting out the conflicts they shared and he asked Sarah for two days so he could think about what she had said. Quietly and sorrowfully she agreed.

Byron respected his father's opinion and went home to talk to him. When Byron arrived back at the farm, Howard realized that his son was troubled. Byron proceeded to pour out his feelings and frustration at Sarah's response to his proposal of marriage.

Howard said he understood women and their emotions. He then went on, as he had many times, to explain how Kathryn represented the virtues of women, who by implication, were above many men. For the first time Byron realized his father was a prisoner to the memory of his late wife and over years he had influenced my view of women. Was he, Byron, a prisoner having the same view of women as his father? Was Sarah similar to his mother? Was he pushing Sarah too hard for a decision when she carried a heavy family burden? Everything was confusing. He was looking for daylight and all he could see was fog.

Then his father said, "Son, do you remember the story in the Book of Genesis about how Jacob had to work seven years to earn the bride price and marry his love, Rachel?"

"Yes, I remembered and have thought about it many times since."

"Did seven years seem like a long time?"

"At times yes, and other times no."

"Well son, there was more to the story than I told you."

Then… he continued. "When Jacob returned after seven years, Laban tricked him, substituting his oldest daughter Leah, whom Jacob married and slept with on his wedding night. When he discovered the exchange, Jacob was angry as he was in love with Rachel, not Leah. Laban told Jacob that by tradition the oldest must be married before the youngest. If he worked another seven years, he could marry Rachel. Jacob did and they were married."

Actually the story was a little different, but like the first time, Howard was trying to make a point. It was not lost on Byron. Howard asked him, "Son, do you love her?"

"Yes, I do."

"Did the seven years pass by quickly?"

"Much of the time, yes."

"What do you have to lose by waiting?"

Byron didn't answer.

As he promised, the next day Byron picked up Sarah at her cottage, but this time he chose a ride in the country rather than along the River Stour. Several miles along a narrow country trail he stopped under an ancient gnarled oak tree surrounded by lush grasslands. A breeze blew through its branches, and leaves fluttered and hummed in the air. When Byron stopped, his horse seemed impatient and took small steps back and forth, rocking as they sat on the trap. An aura of uncertainty surrounded them. Then Byron turned to Sarah and said, "I love you now more than ever and want you to be my wife. I understand the burdens you carry and I am willing to wait."

Sarah was surprised and not sure what to say. She responded, "I want to be your wife and I love you more than ever."

Byron told Sarah he had talked to his father, and had made a decision. He said, "If I waited seven years before, I can wait seven years again."

Sarah was surprised and puzzled. She asked, "What do you mean?"

Byron explained, "Without being your husband, life would be just as lonely here in Shillingstone as anywhere else in the world."

Sarah suddenly knew what he meant and she screamed aloud, "You can't go!"

Byron said nothing more. He slapped the horse's reigns and with a *"click, click",* they rode back to town in silence. Even with a blanket wrapped around her, Sarah was cold and shivered all the way home. When they arrived at her cottage Byron told her he would let her know his plans in several days. She kissed him on the cheek and quietly said, "I love you and thank you."

In Shillingstone there were two young people whose minds continued to be muddled. Sarah again struggled over her obligation to care for her father and mother. Her father's accident had made it worse. He was so thankful that the best daughter in the world would take care of him. Sarah felt hopeless. She could not decide what to do.

Byron no longer had any doubts. He had made his decision that he would rejoin a regiment of the Dragoon Guard Light Horse Cavalry at Camp Aldershot. He told his father, and later, Sergeant Wilson. Finally he visited with Sarah in her cottage and told her of his plan. When Sarah first saw Byron she felt momentary joy. Then on hearing his decision, she was distraught. "What could I do to convince him to stay?" She knew the answer, but she couldn't say it. She sat down on an old chair and cried. Across the room her father sat in his chair, ignoring them both. Only the sounds of her sobbing were heard. Byron suggested they go for a walk and silently Sarah nodded in agreement.

Walking beside each other they proceeded down Poplar Hill toward Blandford Road. As they walked, they were only aware of the sounds of nature and of their feet crunching on the gravel road. They proceeded to Blandford Road and walked across to Church Road. They continued past Church House and left on a path through the kissing gate which led to the cemetery and the Church of the Holy Rood. As usual, the church was open. Byron took Sarah's hand and guided her to his pew, inviting her to sit beside him. This had not been planned. They sat in silence staring at the chancel where couples stood before the vicar to be married. An atmosphere of uncertainty filled the inner sanctum of the church. Both felt uneasy. Then Byron took Sarah's hand and said, "Someday we will be married in this church." Then he proceeded to tell her of his plan to leave in several days.

She could only say, "I am sorry you have to leave." Moments later they returned to Sarah's cottage, but Byron did not go in, pausing only long enough to give her a gentle kiss.

Two days later, Byron, his father, Sarah and her Aunt Edith waited for the Dorset Central train. No one was happy. There were long periods of silence before the train whistle was heard. Edith whispered in Sarah's ear, "It's not too late." Prior to boarding the train Byron had embraced Sarah and promised that he would return. She whispered her love for him. After shaking his father's hand, he boarded the train for Camp Aldershot. With puffing steam and a shrill whistle, the engine chugged down the tracks and out of sight. In the depth of her soul Sarah wondered if she would ever see him again.

ALDERSHOT III

When Byron had entered Camp Aldershot eight years earlier he was just a red-haired farm boy and a raw naïve recruit. He now entered as a veteran lieutenant having fought battles in India and China. Commander Sir John Pennefather welcomed him back and was pleased that he had a seasoned officer on base, able to help in the administration and training of new recruits.

An assistant to Prime Minister Henry Temple had informed General Pennefather that Queen Victoria wished to celebrate the tenth anniversary of Camp Aldershot with a Trooping of the Colours. It was a singular honor as this pageant had been held every year at Buckingham Palace since 1784. The Prime Minister also wished to celebrate the queen's birthday at the same time. The Queen had a deep emotional connection to the camp, as it was a favorite project of her late husband Albert. This would also be a way of honoring Prince Albert for the vision he had for Camp Aldershot. Commander Pennefather and camp personnel were ebullient at the prospect of Trooping the Colours, honoring Albert and simultaneously celebrating Her Majesty's birthday.

For over a century Trooping the Colours had been a military demonstration held annually to observe a sovereign's birthday. Londoners by the thousands flocked to Buckingham Palace to watch a military spectacle and honor their Queen's birthday. Because it was in a different location plans were made to transport up to fifty thousand Londoners the fifty miles to Camp Aldershot.

One of the highlights of the celebration was a concluding twenty-one gun salute to the queen. Unfortunately base gunners were new recruits and not skilled for this assignment. To train these gunners Commander Pennefather appointed Byron as temporary officer in command of the Army Horse Artillery. No one on base had more knowledge or experience than him. With a large number of soldiers on the parade ground there was not enough space for twenty-one units so Byron decided on seven horse artillery units, each firing three times. He had less than forty-five days to train thirty-five gunners and eighty-four horses. With enthusiasm and discipline, Lieutenant Fletcher taught his gunners to become a skilled corps of horse artillery men. Under his command they would be proud and ready to perform their duty.

Early in the morning on the second Friday of June in 1865, thousands of Londoners flocked to Camp Aldershot by train and horse carriages. By mid-morning the royal train from London arrived with Queen Victoria and her entourage. Her Majesty was assisted to her royal landau and proceeded to the parade ground. On the way she was serenaded with military music from the army's brass band. In dress uniforms and regimental formations, five thousand soldiers waited for the queen's arrival and inspection. At the entrance to the parade ground her landau was momentarily halted as the Regimental Commander shouted, "Three cheers for her Majesty Queen Victoria!"

In unison five thousand men shouted at the top of their voices, "Hip hip hooray, hip hip hooray, hip hip hooray!"

She waved in appreciation as her landau wound its way through the formations to inspect each regimental unit. Following her troop inspection she was driven to a reviewing platform where she would have a better view of marching formations and displays of regimental flags.

As the band played Schubert's "Three Marches Militaire," regimental units displayed an impressive variety of precision formations and drills. One unit marched with a row of ten soldiers which merged with another unit, ultimately making one straight line of fifty solders marching in a single line as straight as an arrow. They then moved in a complete circle maintaining a perfectly straight line from the first soldier to the last. Additional marching drills continued with remarkable precision.

Following these drills, regiments were cued to troop their colours and salute the queen as they marched past her viewing stand. First came the queen's mounted band playing "The British Grenadiers" with lead musicians on white horses beating kettle drums attached to each side of their saddles. Remaining band members rode alternating white and black horses while playing their brass instruments. Next came marching regiments of foot soldiers with shouldered rifles following their color bearers. The queen's own Highland Infantry proudly followed their piercing bagpipers playing "Cock O' The North," while kilts fluttered in the wind as they saluted the queen with their colours.

The army band changed music and played Beethoven's "March for Military Band." The last to present their colors was the Queen's Mounted Horse Life Guard Cavalry in their magnificent uniforms atop their magnificent mounts. Riding a beautiful black horse, each officer was dressed in a short scarlet tunic with golden breastplate and Roman helmet adorned with a white horsehair plume. Swords were shouldered by officers wearing white leather gauntlets. Winged black leather jackboots covered most of the riders' slender white leggings as they trotted proudly past the viewing stand saluting Her Majesty, Queen Victoria. They were a majestic display of authority and beauty in the multi-colored pageant.

With a loud thunder of hooves, the Royal Horse Artillery galloped on to the parade ground and saluted the queen as they dashed by the viewing platform. They continued to a distant side of the field and lined up for a twenty-one gun salute. When ready, Lieutenant Fletcher commanded: "Fire!" Every ten seconds a single cannon belched with a thunderous boom and cloud of smoke until the twenty-first shot was fired.

In conclusion, all officers and soldiers stood at attention as the army band struck up the music for "God Save the Queen" and five thousand male voices enthusiastically sang the hymn: "God save our gracious queen, long live our noble queen, God save the queen." A moment of silence followed. Queen Victoria was visibly impressed with the military pageantry and loyalty of her men in uniform. The army band played additional music, soldiers stood at attention, and the

Queen took her royal landau to the train station for the trip to London and Buckingham Palace.

When she left the parade ground the commander shouted, "Stand easy." After a pause he shouted, "Dismissed."

It was an impressive display of Trooping the Colours.

The next morning the base commander congratulated Byron on training the Horse Artillery and the precision of the twenty-one gun salute. As a reward for his leadership and success he was promoted to Captain in the Dragoon Guard Light Horse Cavalry. He was given permission to select a horse from the base stable, and to make an appointment with the tailor for a new uniform.

The army base kept a large stable of horses on the outskirts of the camp. Among a row of horses was a chestnut-colored stallion that stood out from the others. He was a pure-pedigreed Arabian with a chiseled head, long arching neck and high tail carriage. He radiated energy, courage and nobility. When separated from the herd he frolicked around like a young colt. Byron had selected his mount and a name would come later.

All the pieces of Byron's rank came together with his uniform and the selection of his mount. As captain he wore a scarlet waist tunic with gold sleeve braiding, a shoulder epaulette with two silver bars as rank of captain, navy trousers with a red stripe, tall black jackboots with spurs, and white gauntlets. On his mount he had an officer's sword and scabbard plus a new carbine slung on his saddle. His helmet was gilded metal with a white horsehair plume. On horseback Byron was a majestic officer of the Dragoon Guard Light Horse Cavalry. He felt at home.

Back in Shillingstone Sarah's life was not going well. After a month her father had made little improvement. He was impatient and demanded constant attention. Edward believed it was the duty of a daughter to take care of him. Managing her mother was not much easier. Sarah felt she had no life and no Byron. Many nights she cried herself to sleep wondering what she could have done differently. Would Byron be safe? Would she ever see him again? Would her life be better if she had said yes and married Byron? She was morose and silent from guilt.

Byron's Arabian stallion still had not been named when an unlikely source came to mind. Byron attended church faithfully at the base chapel as he had at home. He decided to ask the chaplain to help. Would he know of a Greek or Hebrew name that would mean "fast" or "swift?" Fortunately the chaplain had both a Greek and Hebrew lexicon and agreed to see what he could find. After several weeks he got Byron's attention following a Sunday service. Perhaps he had found a name. He said, "I found the name 'Boaz' in Hebrew which means "Swift." He asked, "Would that describe your horse?

Byron knew immediately it was a great name. Soon the names of Byron and Boaz were almost synonymous. Every morning Byron rode Boaz around the base for an hour and then back to the camp stable to wash and brush him down. He would regularly stop by in the evening and talk to the animal, and just enjoyed his presence. He had never before experienced such a bond between a man and a horse. There would be times when his life would depend on a bond with this fast and agile steed.

At twenty-nine, Captain Byron Fletcher was the senior officer on the base and an assistant to the commander. He trained cavalry officers in horsemanship, gunnery, cavalry formations, all military commands, as well as military discipline. He was well-liked and often told mesmerizing stories of battle over a pint in the officers' club.

Toward the end of Byron's first year back at Camp Aldershot, the base commander had a new assignment for him and twenty-five of his fellow cavalry officers. They were being assigned to duty in New Zealand, a place none had ever heard of before. Prior to departure they were given a seventy-two hour leave. Upon returning they were to prepare for a two-month passage to New Zealand. In route they would receive further information on their assignment.

With a leave of only three days, Byron decided to surprise Sarah and take the Dorset Central Railway to Shillingstone. He arrived in late evening and decided to stay overnight at the Old Ox Inn. Much to Byron's disappointment, for some unknown reason, Sergeant Wilson was away for several days. However, he would be well rested and would see Sarah in the morning.

When Byron knocked at her front door Sarah almost fainted. She was shocked and embarrassed, as the cottage was not tidy. She was both excited and nervous, unsure why he had come. She gave him a warm embrace and offered him tea. Sarah sipped her tea on a bench at the kitchen table and stared at Byron. Conversation was awkward. He wanted her to know that in two days he would be sailing thousands of miles away to New Zealand. He would always be thinking of her and would write often. They embraced and he left. A well-intended surprise resulted in a letdown. The quandary in her life appeared to be unchanged.

Byron spent the rest of the day with his father. They talked about everything. Byron told him about choosing an Arabian horse, trooping the colors and his assignment to New Zealand. As a farmer with livestock, Howard wanted to know more about his Arabian horse. It turned out to be one of the best visits Byron ever had with his father. On the following morning, Howard hitched up the trap and took his son to the train depot for the return trip to camp. Waiting on the platform they continued their conversation until the station master shouted, "Dorset Central Railway arriving for passengers going east." Although he had invited Sarah to see him off she could not bring herself to watch him leave. Byron scanned the platform and could not find her. He was disappointed she had not come to say good bye.

NEW ZEALAND

When Byron and his men arrived at Portsmouth waiting dockside was the HMS Lord Warden, a sail-steamer that would take them to New Zealand. She was a stout ship with a speed of 13.5 knots under steam and 10 knots under sail. The ship's company included 605 sailors and officers, plus twenty-five cavalry soldiers and their mounts.

On the last day of September, 1866, the good ship HMS Lord Warden cast off her moorings and steamed out of Portsmouth naval harbor to the open sea for a 15,000 nautical mile trip to New Zealand. Sailing time was estimated at 60 to 70 days.

Other than the name New Zealand, none of the cavalry officers knew its location or importance. For a month HMS Warden sailed south along the coast of Africa to Cape Colony where the ship took on coal and fresh provisions. Back at sea the HMS Lord Warden rounded the Cape of Good Hope and established an easterly bearing toward Australia. They sailed south below Australia and continued toward New Zealand. With their destination weeks away, all cavalry officers were instructed to gather in the ships ward room for information on their destination. Chief Warrant Officer Walker had sailed there twice and was acquainted with the north island of New Zealand.

When they were assembled he explained, "Gentlemen, New Zealand consists of two large islands, the larger South island and the North Island. Our destination is the city of

Auckland on the west side of the North Island. The native population are known as Maori, who have a reputation as fierce tattooed warriors. Since 1840 the English and Maori had been at war. Recently, fighting has increased and the conflict needs to be resolved." In conclusion, Officer Walker told them, "Gentlemen, this is why you are here."

In the middle of December, 1866, a shout of "Land ho!" descended from the crow's nest. Soon Byron and his comrades could see the islands of New Zealand spread across the horizon. As the ship came closer, beautiful islands rose up in front of them with a deep green forest of trees that appeared to float on the blue Tasmanian Sea. The reality of Auckland harbor was less appealing. They found it cluttered with floating debris and the rotting remains of old sailing ships, reminiscent of a frontier anchorage.

The HMS Lord Warden docked near a commercial section close to town. Disembarking began immediately and would continue into the next day. An officer in charge of the port informed Byron that there was a military stockade a mile inland that might function as a temporary base for his officers and livestock.

With the assistance of local stevedores the ship's crew gathered enough wagons for the cavalry to get their mounts, equipment, ammunition, and supplies to Waitara, a place that could charitably be called an army camp. By anyone's standard it was primitive. Barracks were poorly constructed shacks, the mess hall was miniscule, and the parade ground was nothing more than a patch of fine red dirt. Little provision was made for animal stock, apart from a flimsy wire fence. A stray cow could have casually walked through the camp unimpeded.

As officer in command, Byron decided his first order of business was to find the camp commander and request improvements. He was informed that the major responsible for the camp was on the south island and it was unknown when he would return.

Clearly it would be impossible to have a military presence without a base from which to operate. Captain Byron assembled his officers and formed a plan to rebuild the base. Next he went to the Government House and received authority to build the camp. In six weeks the Calvary officers had built a facility with comfortable barracks, a large well-equipped mess hall, and a new firm gravel parade ground. In the middle of the camp they planted a flag pole to display a large Union Jack. A sizable pasture with a secure fence was built as well as a new stable for their horses. Byron was proud of their work and renamed it Blandford Base, after the main road in his home village of Shillingstone.

Several weeks passed before Byron checked for mail at the post office. Waiting for him were four letters from Sarah. He read the one on top.

> *My dear Byron: By now you are likely in New Zealand. It may be different than the land here at home. My mother is in failing health, is bedridden and dependent on her*

medicine more than ever. My father spends most of his time working seventy miles away in Shrewsbury. I am very lonely and miss you. Time seems to move slowly and I have difficulty believing how long it will be before you return. I love you and miss you terribly. Sarah

Setting that letter aside he read the next one.

Dear Byron: I haven't received a letter from you in a long time. I stop at the post office every day hoping for a letter from you. Nothing has changed with my mother and father. We had some excitement here as the Prince of Wales came to our train station for a hunting weekend. Your father came by the cottage and said he got a letter from you and that you were safe and very busy. I feel alone and continue to be stuck in the cottage much of the time. I yearn for you to be here with me. With all my love, Sarah.

Byron read her other letters and they were much the same. Since Byron left home he had traveled thousands of miles, more than halfway around the world. During the same time Sarah had moved no more than a few miles in any direction from her cottage and every day was predictable.

With Blandford Base complete, serious training began. After two months at sea and almost two months building Blandford Base some cavalry skills had diminished for both men and mounts. Captain Byron implemented an arduous regimen to get his units in battle-ready condition. Orders for deployment had not yet arrived, and no clear chain of command had come from the government.

Sarah's mother took up a good part of the morning to get her day started. In midafternoon Sarah, as usual, visited the post office, then bought necessities from the bake shop and green grocer. Along the way she was greeted by neighbors who asked about her mother and Byron but showed little interest in her life. Sarah's only time for herself came after supper when Mildred was in bed and many times she would read herself to sleep. Other evenings all she could think about was Byron. When would he return? Would he be the same person? Would he still love her?

In Sarah's daily activity her mother was an unpredictable factor. Most of the time Mildred's mood swung from deep guilt and gloominess to euphoria. There would be long periods with no conversation and then suddenly she would not stop talking about Christopher and how she wished he had never been born. Only a swig of laudanum settled her down. More than once, Sarah wondered if she would be like her mother. She hoped that would never happen.

One morning Mildred didn't respond when Sarah called her. Thinking her mother was still asleep she decided to let her sleep. Later when Sarah checked on her she was still sleeping, or was she? While she looked calm and restful, when Sarah touched her cheek it was cold. Sarah suddenly realized that her mother was dead. Shaken, she leaned over to confirm this fact and her foot kicked something on the floor. It was an empty laudanum bottle. Last evening it had been half full, but now it was empty. What had happened? Sarah had no answer other than her mother was dead and she didn't know what to do.

Aunt Edith was the only person she could think of for help. After crying all the way to Edith's cottage, Sarah told her what had happened. Edith was not surprised. She comforted Sarah, suggesting they return to her cottage and decide what to do next. Sarah thought Reverend Dayman would know what to do. While Edith stayed at the cottage, Sarah walked to the rectory. Reverend Dayman saw that Sarah was obviously in shock and grieving. He invited her in and then asked his wife for tea. Sobbing, Sarah explained her situation and now didn't know what to do. Hot tea soothed her emotions and Reverend Dayman explained steps that needed to be taken. First the body must be washed, then dressed in fresh clothes and laid out on her bed. He offered to contact Mrs. Mumford to assist in her mother's preparation. Then he asked, "Where is your father?"

Sarah cried, "I don't know."

He added, "Perhaps you could have his company find him and let him know about the death of his wife. Ask them to send him home quickly."

"I shall, as soon as possible."

On his own, Reverend Dayman asked the village carpenter to make a coffin. Then he asked Mrs. Haggardy to assist Sarah with the funeral arrangements. She was pleased to help.

Just after the noon hour Mrs. Mumford arrived at Sarah's cottage with an armload of clean rags, body oil and soap. It seems she was involved in the lives of those both arriving and departing. She had prepared as many bodies in death as she had assisted in births. She took charge and asked Sarah for warm water, clean underclothing, a clean dress, clean sheets, a clean pillow case and a blanket. Fortunately Mildred's eyes and mouth were closed. To be sure her mouth stayed closed Mrs. Mumford placed a ribbon of cloth under Mildred's chin and tied it firmly to the top of her head. With some string she tied Mildred's big toes together so her legs would not separate from rigor mortis. After the body was washed, dressed and placed on a blanket on her bed, Sarah's mother was ready to be reviewed.

Mildred died on Tuesday morning, and a funeral needed be held within four days. When all arrangements were complete, a service was scheduled for Saturday afternoon at the Church of the Holy Rood. Edward wired that he would be home the following Monday. There was no expression of sadness that his wife had died.

No event, whether birth, death or catastrophe, occurred in Shillingstone without everyone knowing. Almost every space in the Church of the Holy Rood was filled on Saturday afternoon. Reverend Dayman offered a comforting eulogy about Mildred and gave an appropriate homily for the occasion. He read from Psalms, "For his anger lasts only for a moment, but his favor lasts a lifetime; weeping may stay for a night, but rejoicing comes in the morning." Then from Matthew: "Blessed are those who mourn, for they shall be comforted."

Following the service, pallbearers carried the coffin to a prepared cemetery plot. Mourners followed the vicar to the site and he read, "For as much as it please almighty God to remove from this world the soul of our sister, we lay her body here to rest awhile, then to be buried in the ground, then shall the dust turn to dust, but the spirit returns to Almighty God who gave it. Amen."

Guests were invited to Sarah's cottage for refreshments provided by Mrs. Haggardy. As much as she wished to attend, there was a question about whether or not the door was adequate for her passage. It was not. Neighbors, friends, church members and shopkeepers stopped by and shared memories of Mildred. Their presence was comforting for both Sarah and her Aunt Edith.

When Edward returned on Monday afternoon Sarah refused to talk to him.

MAORI

A year before Captain Fletcher and his comrades arrived in New Zealand in 1866, Auckland was the capital and Sir George Grey, KCB, had been named governor. Byron had requested a meeting with the governor to clarify his assignment in this new country. Sir George complimented Byron as he had received excellent reports of the young man's leadership both in Auckland and from previous military assignments. In short order Byron would understand his mission.

Lord Grey told him, "Captain Fletcher, New Zealand is a different world from India and China. Perhaps some background will help you understand this country." Then he explained that by 1800 many, perhaps hundreds, of whaling ships had been anchoring in New Zealand for water and provisions for over a century. All were greeted by the native population known as Maori, at times in kindly fashion, sometimes by warriors with fearsome tattooed faces, bulging wide eyes and tongues hanging out, after which the newcomers were killed and eaten! Lord Grey continued, "By killing and eating their victims the Maori believe they gain 'mana' or strength."

He told Byron that the first European settlers arrived in 1810 and received a similar reception. Tensions rose as more colonists arrived and took land from the Maori. Conflicts continued until 1840 when the British government negotiated a treaty with Maori chiefs, who accepted New Zealand as a British colony under authority of the Crown.

Since then an uneasy peace had existed. "Recently the Maori revived the belief that they had been cheated and that their land was stolen from them. Near outright war has started again. Regardless of how many Imperial soldiers try, they are unable to subdue the Maori."

The governor also informed Byron that Sir Victor Hamilton, KCB, was the newly-appointed commander of all military operations in New Zealand. His headquarters were in Wellington, and Captain Fletcher would be under Lord Hamilton's command. Furthermore he was informed that Wellington was now the new capital of the country.

Sir George added, "Captain, you need to know the Maori. There is no better person from whom to learn about them than Reverend Richard Davis of the Te Waimate Mission House. His mission was one of the first established in New Zealand north of Auckland. You need to meet him."

Byron answered, "Sir, thank you for your advice. You can be confident the Dragoon Guard Light Horse Cavalry will contribute to the success of the Queen's colony in New Zealand."

When Byron returned to base, a twelve-year-old boy was waiting to give him a note from Auckland's postmaster. The note read, "You need not come to the post office daily to check your mail. If there are letters for you or any officer on your base I will have this young Maori boy deliver them immediately."

When Byron asked the boy his name, he replied, "Matiu." This was Byron's first introduction to a Maori.

A journey north to the Te Waimate Mission would give Byron and Boaz plenty of exercise as it was almost a hundred miles north. Using inland roads and treacherous primitive trails, Byron estimated the trip would take a week or more. Byron talked to his horse about what they would face in New Zealand and that it might not be pleasant. Along the way Boaz neighed, snorted and moved his head up and down, giving the impression that he understood. On a clear stretch of trail Boaz was anxious to run. Encouraged by Byron, he reared up pawing the air with his front legs, snorted and raced ahead for the next three miles. Boaz galloped so fast had Byron to lean forward and hold on tight.

Reverend Richard Davis had been a farmer prior to becoming a missionary. Beautiful landscaping around the mission had the imprint of a farmer's hand. Byron shared that he was the son of a farmer. Te Waimate was the second oldest mission in New Zealand and was well established. If anyone knew the Maori well it was Reverend Davis, who quickly understood the purpose of the Captain's visit. He and his wife were pleased to have Byron as their guest.

After the usual exchange of pleasantries, Reverend Davis described the Maori natives of New Zealand. He explained, "Maori men are large, olive-skinned, with thick black hair similar to Polynesians. Every man has facial tattoos scraped into his skin with ink made of ash and fat. Ownership of land is the core ingredient in a Maori's life." He continued, "Most conflicts with settlers is over possession of land."

135

Across New Zealand Maori were known as savage warriors. The moniker was well-deserved. A fierce tattooed face and body, plus an ear-piercing war whoop were often enough to scare an enemy. Victorious warriors took no prisoners. They cut off survivor's heads and ate their torsos. To preserve an enemy's head, the brain was removed, the eyes and mouth sewn shut, and the head steamed, dried in the sun, and finally coated with shark oil. It was a trophy of war and was kept in a victor's hut.

For centuries Maori warriors fought each other face to face with clubs and spears. A change occurred with the arrival of sailing ships and settlers. Maori were introduced to the European musket and the benefit it provided in battle. About the same time, Europeans discovered tattooed Maori heads, and they became prized as souvenirs. When Maori became aware a tattooed head was treasured by Europeans, they bartered one head for one musket plus ammunition. Over decades hundreds of Maori heads were taken back to countries around the world. Tribes with many heads to barter acquired many muskets, resulting in an uneven balance of power. Those with few muskets were slaughtered, creating more heads to trade. In addition, Maori warriors now had muskets to defend their land from an increasing number of settlers.

Byron stayed overnight at the mission, and in the morning Reverend Davis suggested that he visit a Quaker family fifty miles farther north near the Bay of Islands. He pointed out that this was where most ships landed for provisions and also had the largest population of Maori. Since Quakers appeared to have friendly relations with the Maori, perhaps they could give Byron additional insight into the native culture. Byron was curious how these peace-loving missionaries could survive in such a violent environment and he looked forward to meeting them.

Toward the end of a delightful New Zealand day Captain Fletcher and Boaz reached a small homestead surrounded by large trees, flowering shrubs and a manicured lawn. In the middle was a modest white house with a wraparound porch. As Byron and Boaz approached, Reverend Jabir Blackhouse and his wife, Quieta, stepped out and welcomed him to the Society of Friends Mission. Captain Byron extended a greeting from Reverend Davis and family, and then explained the purpose of his visit. Since it was evening he was invited to stay the night. Before their children were off to bed, Quieta introduced their three young daughters to this tall red-haired cavalry officer. They were excited when Byron told them they could have a ride on Boaz in the morning if they went right to sleep. He was impressed with their manners.

After breakfast the next day Reverend Jabir and Captain Fletcher walked around the mission grounds and Byron asked, "How can a small family of five have any influence on a warrior culture?"

Jabir welcomed the question and replied, "Let me tell you a story. We don't own the land on which we live, it is leased from a local Maori tribe. We had an unresolved issue on our lease agreement so they took all of our sheep, twenty-five in all. When our issues were resolved we expected our sheep to be returned, but they weren't. As Quakers, we said nothing. A year later they were returned."

Byron was curious and asked, "Why did they return your sheep?"

Jabir was delighted to explain, "Well, a basic tenet of our faith is that we believe all humans have an inner light given to them from God. I believe that's why they returned our sheep. That's the reason we're here."

Byron was interested in how successful they were and inquired, "May I ask how many converts you have?"

The Quaker's response was, "Captain, we don't use the word 'convert', we refer to Maori as friends. As Quakers we are a Society of Friends. In contrast, Anglican missionaries baptize their converts. However, to be baptized, a Maori must renounce cannibalism, polygamy, child infanticide and barbaric practices. As our friends we teach them to read, write, farm and become acquainted with our European culture. We believe they will realize their inner light and become children of God."

Byron concluded with a comment, "Now I understand why Reverend Davis suggested a visit to your mission. Thank you for your hospitality. A question before I leave. I met a young Maori at my base in Auckland and he said his name was Matiu. Does his name have any meaning?"

Jabir understood the question and answered, "Indeed it does. In Maori it means 'a gift of God'. Most Maori names have meanings. Captain, my wife Quieta has enjoyed your visit and you are welcome to come again. God bless you on your journey back to Auckland."

After giving the children a ride on Boaz as promised, Byron mounted his horse and started back to Auckland. During the week or so that it would take he tried to absorb differing views of the Maori. On the way he talked out loud to himself as Boaz trotted at a comfortable pace, nodding his head up and down nickering and neighing as usual. Captain Fletcher believed Reverend Jabir was naïve in his view of the Maori and decided to keep informed about the family's safety.

MAJOR BASIL RUTHERFORD

Byron's first stop was the military base. He was welcomed back by his fellow comrades and was informed that they had a new base commander, Major Basil Rutherford. Byron was told to report to the regimental headquarters immediately on returning. After putting Boaz away he was led to the major's office, where before him stood a stubby older officer in full dress uniform with a smartly-trimmed head of thick white hair, a ruddy complexion and a face creased with wrinkles befitting a weathered curmudgeon. Byron saluted confidently and reported, "Captain Byron Fletcher reporting as ordered, sir."

"Yes…yes…yes, finally back! What did you find out about those bloody naked savages?"

"Sir, I was sent by Lord Grey to visit several mission stations and report to the governor on their mission work with the Maori."

"Damn it, Captain, As Major in command of all military units from Auckland and further north you will report only to me! Now Captain what did you find?"

"Sir, I found that they are trying to make them Christians."

"Bloody good that will do. Savages are to be killed, not converted. We've been fighting them for over twenty-five years and we're still fighting. My assignment is to put an end to it. I've fought battles over opium in China, fought in the bloody Crimean war and have prevailed in every battle." He paused for a moment for that to sink in and then continued, "My promotions were not from officer training in Sandhurst, but through the ranks on the battlefield. Now Captain, I want you to take your men and your little ponies and find me some Maori to fight. Report back in seventy-two hours or sooner. Is that understood?"

"Yes, sir!"

As Captain Fletcher left he realized working under this new commander would be difficult. Before meeting Lord Grey he gathered his cavalry together and told them, "I have received our orders and we are to find a Maori encampment." He chose six teams of four riders with provisions for three days in the field. A map indicated areas they were to search.

After he assigned his comrades to their duties, he rode Boaz to the governor's residence to report his visits to the missions. None of Byron's observations on the Maori were new to the governor. Lord Grey expressed appreciation for his report and reminded him that future visits would be in Wellington.

Back at Blandford Base young Matiu ran after Byron and gave him two letters from England. The date on the first letter indicated it was written six months ago. As usual Byron was pleased to get them and found a quiet place to read.

My dear Byron, My mother continues to be the burden of my life. She is sick, emotional and demanding. I asked my father to help but he tells me I should be grateful for the years he spent as my tutor and that he pays the bills. He said his responsibility ends there. Every day is much the same. Most of the time I feel lonely. One bright spot was an invitation for afternoon tea from Mrs. Gertrude Haggardy along with three other village ladies. For the first time I got to meet several other women I had previously known only by name. I am sorry for my past decision to delay our marriage, but I look forward to your return when we can be husband and wife. My life will finally be fulfilled. I pray daily that you will be safe. Your dearest Sarah

Byron reread some of Sarah's old letters and they were quite similar. She was unhappy and her life was the same every day. It was somewhat difficult to have a lot of sympathy for Sarah when he had faced life and death challenges.

Before leaving Auckland for Wellington, Captain Fletcher asked Major Rutherford for more time in their search for the Maori as distances were considerable and travel difficult. He was granted a week. For the first time Byron realized the difficulty of his assignment. A road to Wellington did not exist, only trails through valleys and dense forests. Most travel was by coastal steamers. As soon as possible Byron arranged passage on a steamer for himself and Boaz. Even then it would take a full day as it sailed down the coast.

Wellington was a beautiful harbor city surrounded by lush tree-lined hills. Government house was a large white frame building sitting on the side of a hill a short distance from the harbor. After departing the coastal steamer, Byron and Boaz made their way along dirt roads to the government building to meet Lord Grey. His secretary indicated the governor was away, but the new military commander, General Sir Victor Hamilton was in an office down the hall. In meeting General Hamilton Byron saluted and said, "Sir, Captain Byron Fletcher of the Dragoon Guard Light Horse Cavalry present on orders from Major Rutherford to locate Maori villages and camps."

"Captain, thank you for coming to Wellington and introducing yourself. I understand you have served with distinction and I am pleased to meet you. We do have challenges with the Maori population as over 90 percent are located in the north of this island. Conflicts with them continue and Major Rutherford had been assigned to resolve the situation. There are four thousand Imperial soldiers sailing to Auckland under his command to facilitate this objective. Your assignment is to assist Major Rutherford and report back on progress as soon as possible."

Byron responded, "Sir, I consider it an honor to be here and will serve to the best of my ability."

With that part of the mission completed, Byron made his way to the harbor with Boaz and boarded the first coastal steamer to Auckland. At Blandford Base he assembled his comrades and received their reports. No significant assembly of Maori was observed except in the Bay of Islands. They had heard reports of an Anglican missionary who had sided with Maori tribes to resist the Crown. Further interviews named him as Scotsman Angus McGill, a soldier and clergyman who now lived with the Maori. Byron decided to follow this lead and determine if the fellow was a threat.

After he reported his findings to Major Rutherford, he asked permission to take three comrades with him to the village of Paihia on the shore of The Bay of Islands. At first the major refused, but Byron prevailed and asked for one week to investigate, prior to any military encounter. Permission was granted.

Within a day Byron and three of his fellow cavalry officers and their mounts were on a coastal steamer sailing 120 miles north to the Bay of Islands. Byron viewed some of the most beautiful scenery he had ever seen. Entering the harbor to the village of Paihia he saw a pristine sand beach interspersed with numerous fascinating rock formations leading up to hills covered with lush bushes and flowers.

Further on there were endless stands of tall trees on elevated ground which Byron later learned was known as Russell Forest. A short distance from shore lay a small village of about a dozen buildings. The four men and mounts ventured into the village to seek information about a Scottish man in the area, but no one had heard of him, or maybe was unwilling to say. Then Byron remembered that Reverend Davis Mission was about fifteen miles inland from Paihia.

Reverend Davis and his family were delighted to see Captain Fletcher and his fellow officers. Byron explained the purpose of his visit: "A large population of Maori lives around the Bay of Islands and the governor was concerned that conflicts might arise over the price and purchase of land. I understand a Scotsman is gathering Maori to contest the sale of their land. Do you know anything about him?"

Reverend Davis was willing to share what he knew, "Indeed I do...his name is Angus McGill. From my information he was a soldier with the British army fighting in the Opium Wars in China. He was repulsed by the carnage and greed of the English. When his enlistment was complete he decided to enter the ministry and was assigned to a small Anglican mission called Cape Regina on the tip of North Island. At first he had some mission success until he learned that some Maori had been killed by the English in a land grab. He came to believe that the English were the same here as in China. Indications are that he left his mission to live with a Maori tribe and there he took up their cause against the English. Rumblings of a conflict have been heard, but nothing has happened yet."

"Your information has been helpful, Reverend Davis. Let us hope that armed conflict can be avoided."

Captain Fletcher and his fellow cavalry men rode back to Paihia and took the same steamer back to Auckland. With their mounts back in their stalls at Blandford Camp he reported to Major Rutherford. When Byron entered regimental headquarters he was immediately ushered into the major's office. His superior immediately blurted out, "By God, I hope you have some good news for me. Do they want a fight?"

Captain Byron answered, "Sir, I have no information that they are prepared to fight. Most of the island is calm with the exception of the northern end where most Maori live. There have been some gatherings around the leadership of a Scotsman named Angus McGill."

The major's face flushed red and he cried out, "Angus McGill, you say, McGill?"

"Yes sir, apparently a soldier in the British army who fought in India and China."

By now the major's body was so flushed with anger that he appeared about to explode and he shouted, "McGill...I know him...I know him...he fought under me in China, a bloody lazy scoundrel. What the hell is he doing here?"

Byron replied, "Sir, when he returned to England he entered the ministry and had a mission on the north end of the island. Apparently he identified with the Maori cause

146

who believed their land had been unfairly confiscated. Some Maori were killed by the English."

The Major couldn't contain himself and cried out, "He's trouble. He's trouble. Always trouble. Just wait, there'll be discord now. Captain, put the base on high alert and be prepared for any conflict on a moment's notice."

Byron thought it strange that the major knew McGill. He must have been a real problem in China. In any event, Byron had an assignment for the garrison to be on high alert and ready to be mobilized on a moment's notice. After several days of activity, he informed the major that the base would be ready to mobilize upon his order.

WAR

Within a month conflict erupted. Near his former mission McGill and ten Maori warriors chopped down a flagpole flying the Union Jack. The group then started south waving the flag in defiance against the Crown. Along the way additional Maori joined the group. By the time they had gone fifty miles farther south the group had grown to over a hundred Maori. At this site McGill set up a temporary camp and challenged the English to come and retrieve their flag. With no response the Maori went on a rampage, killing colonists and missionaries in the area. By the time they reached the Quaker mission they had slaughtered sixty-seven innocent men, women and children.

Early in the conflict Byron received a report on what had happened to the Quaker family. Reverend Jabir and Quieta had heard Maori warriors shouting outside their mission house and they stepped off the porch to greet them. In moments they were attacked with clubs and spears and perished. Several Maori then entered the mission house and slaughtered their three beautiful children. Their bodies lay on the front lawn, beaten beyond recognition. Byron was not surprised by the attack, but shocked that they had killed and mutilated the bodies of the entire family.

News of the massacre filtered back to Auckland. When Major Rutherford was informed of the butchery he was livid. He shouted, "By God and country, I'll take care of those heathens in quick order." He commanded Captain Fletcher to have his cavalry prepared to embark in twelve hours along with an army of fifteen hundred soldiers. Five coastal steamers had been put on standby and were now prepared to embark. All personnel, horses, equipment and provisions were loaded on the steamers which set sail for the village of Paihia on the shore of the Bay of Islands.

Two days after Major Rutherford was informed of the killings, five steamers arrived at the Paihia. The Major instructed Byron to take his cavalry and search for the Maori encampment, while other soldiers were assigned to build a secure base camp.

Some 20 miles from Paihia Angus McGill and his Maori warriors had established a camp surrounded by a wooden palisade. Being an experienced soldier, McGill instructed his warriors in the use of their muskets in combat. Following the massacre, there was no question that they would be doing battle with the Imperial Army. It was only a question of when and where. A few Maori, sympathetic to their cause, kept McGill informed on movements of the English army.

Three Light Horse Cavalry men returned with news of the Maori camp's location. It was tucked in a dense forest and protected by a wooden palisade. They estimated that 200 warriors were in the camp. A rough map had been drawn for the major indicating the camp's location. With 1,500 solders under his command, Major Rutherford announced that he would attack the enemy and wipe them off the face of the earth.

His plan was to attack straight on with a volley of musket fire followed by a charge with fixed bayonets, and shoot his way into the enclosure, killing all the remaining Maori. Byron informed him the trail to the palisade was narrow; only two soldiers could fight shoulder to shoulder. Some distance from the camp's location, Byron suggested that when they arrive they should spread out and create a long deep line for a frontal attack.

Looking at him with disgust the Major declared, "Captain, who's in charge of this campaign?"

"Sir, you are, sir!"

"Then you and your pony will be lead scout, and I will follow and lead a charge against the enemy. Is that clear?"

"Yes, sir."

Captain Fletcher was uneasy as he rode Boaz a short distance ahead of Major Rutherford and his soldiers. Even Boaz was uneasy and sniffed the air, moving his head back and forth sensing others were on the trail. His senses were correct.

A mile from the Maori camp all hell broke loose. It was an ambush. Musket fire came from both sides of the trail. Major Rutherford was the first to fall, perhaps shot by McGill. His soldiers quickly fell from volley after volley of musket shot from the forest. Others retreated in panic.

When he heard firing, Byron turned Boaz around and returned to find the major. He had been seriously wounded but he was still alive. Byron quickly pulled him up behind him in the saddle and rode Boaz out of the action. At a safe distance he gave instructions to a sergeant to take Boaz and the major back to camp. On a fresh horse he returned to the fight. Byron shouted for his soldiers to lie down and shoot, load on their backs, turn over and shoot again. He rode back and forth along the line, rallying his troops. Miraculously he was not hit. Two thirds of the troops retreated back to camp. Others not killed or wounded fought on until the shooting ended. Having accomplished their mission, the Maori warriors slipped into the bush and disappeared.

Captain Fletcher rode among the troops to check their status, then rapidly rode back to camp. Once there he ordered a group of soldiers to return to the scene of battle and collect the dead and wounded. It was a catastrophe.

Back at camp Byron checked on Major Rutherford. He had been shot three times, with wounds to the side of his head, the right side of his chest and left leg above the knee. Likely the major would survive and retire from the army. As senior officer Captain Fletcher assumed command. His first command was to send all but 1,000 troops back to Auckland along with the wounded. Later he counted 36 soldiers dead, 63 wounded and 12 Maori bodies recovered. Now in command he began reviewing his unpleasant options.

While Maori warriors were in the minority, they had similar weapons, they had intimate knowledge of the territory and were highly motivated to fight. They were fierce warriors and New Zealand belonged to them. In contrast, the English military were enforcers of government policy with little incentive to fight. Captain Fletcher concluded that fighting the Maori would drag on for some time, but his immediate duty was with an existing conflict.

Byron felt he had nothing to lose by taking a white flag to the Maori camp and measuring their intentions. When his camp in Paihia was in order, he took six comrades with him to the Maori encampment. As he approached with a white flag, Angus McGill strutted out the front gate. He was a short, burly Scotsman with sharp facial features and menacing recessed eyes. Byron dismounted and stated his purpose in coming: "Mr. McGill, allow me to inform you that Major Rutherford was severely wounded, but will survive. I understand that you and he are acquainted and have adverse opinions of each other."

McGill responded in anger, "The stupidity of that bastard had cost many a soldier his life. He deserves what he got, and more."

"I was hoping there might be a way to resolve this conflict, or at least give us time to work on a resolution. What say you?"

"Do I understand you wish to seek peace? It's not possible unless the government gives back land owned by the Maori."

"Mr. McGill, there are some factors that give you and the Maori an advantage. But you well know that over time, this is a war of attrition. You know it means the Maori will lose, if not now, then in the future. Those who stay on a sinking ship long enough go down with it."

"It's too late. Maori tribes are seeking retribution and will settle for nothing less."

"Actually, Mr. McGill, you have given the colonists a gift. Up to now the English have fought out of duty to the Crown. Now that innocents have been slaughtered, you have ignited a passion for revenge. You will lose. In addition, you will either die in battle or hang for the innocents you have killed. I refer specifically to the peace-loving Quaker family who were killed and mutilated. Good day, sir."

No further comments came from McGill. As Captain Fletcher mounted Boaz, McGill turned back and entered the stockade a little less arrogant than when he came out.

When Byron arrived back at Camp Paihia he had a decision to make. He could wait for a response from McGill or he could make a surprise attack. He chose the latter and it would begin the next morning. During the afternoon he assembled 500 soldiers and 12 of his comrades. In the dark of night 150 soldiers would circle through the woods ready to attack the right flank of the camp, and a similar number would attack the left flank. The remaining soldiers would charge the front gate when the Maori came out to fight. On the sound of cannon the battle would begin.

Captain Fletcher had brought a small eight-pound artillery piece that had been left at the Blandford Base. It was small enough to be pulled down a trail to the Maori camp. He had three eight-pound balls to discharge and sufficient gun powder. It would suffice, as a direct shot would blow open the front gate. With the precision of an experienced gunner he set up the artillery piece 300 yards from the front gate and fired the cannon. The cannon's boom surprised the Maori and blew the gate to pieces. The battle began.

Running to escape, the Maori were mowed down by a volley of fire from five hundred muskets. Spreading out they were shot or fell to the bayonet. In a few minutes the fighting was over, with many dead and wounded Maori on the ground. Remaining Maori fighters vanished into the forest, as did McGill. Eighty-one Maori were dead or wounded with seven British soldiers dead and nine wounded. Morale among the English forces increased dramatically.

Byron returned to Auckland with the dead and wounded. When he entered Blandford Base he was welcomed back a hero. He had saved the major's life and had returned to take command of the remaining soldiers. He had successfully won an important battle against the Maori camp.

Young Matiu delivered two letters to Byron from Sarah. Both had been written more than three months earlier. In the quiet of the commander's office he read the earliest first.

My dear Byron:

I find it difficult to write this letter as my mother recently died in her sleep. It was a shock when I discovered that she had died. I am beyond grief. I didn't know what to do. I talked to Reverend

Dayman and along with Edith they guided me through the funeral. As usual my father was not home and did not get home until a day after the funeral. I was so angry that I refused to speak to him. All this made me anxious. Knowing of your love brought some balm to my frayed emotions. I love you dearly and wish you were here beside me. All my love, Sarah.

By the second letter, her mood had improved.

Dearest Byron:

I feel bad for crying about the death of my mother. Please forgive me. I feel much better now. Edith has been a great support. She is so different from my mother. On a trip to the post office, I met the new blacksmith, a fellow by the name of Andy Dunn. He asked if I needed any repairs to my cottage. I let him know I needed new door hinges and a new door latch. In two days the job was done. We chatted for a while and he reminded me of you. It made me feel better. Keep safe and know you have all my love. Sarah.

Sarah: I have just finished reading both your recent letters. You have all my sympathy on the death of your mother and hope your Aunt Edith will continue to provide succor. Your story about meeting the new blacksmith sounds like your life may be beginning to get back to normal. Here on base our comrades rally around those who have been injured. Time continues to move on and it brings me closer to when I return to Shillingstone and we can be married. With affection, Byron.

A SPECIAL HONOR

When Captain Fletcher arrived back at his base in Auckland he was asked to meet with the new army commander, General Hamilton, at his headquarters in Wellington. No sense of urgency was implied by the invitation. Byron expressed appreciation for the invitation and responded with the day he would arrive. He then booked passage on a coastal steamer for Wellington

On arrival the captain proceeded to the general's headquarters. He was ushered in by the secretary announcing, "Sir, Captain Byron Fletcher, as you requested."

The general greeted him enthusiastically: "Well, well, Captain Fletcher, you have cut a wide swath of success in a short time. I am impressed, but I will let others list your accomplishments. I have a reason for inviting you here, but Governor Grey asked that you visit him first."

"Yes, sir, I will be pleased to do so."

"I was also invited to the meeting with the governor and you are welcome to ride with me to Parliament House".

On arrival the general guided him to the governor's office where they found it crowded with many of New Zealand's political leaders. He was warmly greeted by the governor who began a speech to those assembled: "Gentlemen, it is an honor to have Captain Byron Fletcher in my office today. He saved the life of his commander, Major Rutherford, took over command and led his soldiers into battle. Further, he planned and executed a successful raid on a Maori camp. It is my honor as Governor of New Zealand and as the representative of Queen Victoria to award this prestigious medal, the Victoria Cross, to Captain Byron Fletcher for valor in the face of the enemy." After extended applause he continued, "Now, what say you?"

Byron didn't know what to say. It was a complete surprise. After a thoughtful pause he said, "Governor, this is unexpected and I am not sure it is deserved, but I accept this honor on behalf of my comrades with the Dragoon Guard Light Horse Cavalry and the great soldiers of the British army. Thank you." His speech was followed by boisterous applause. The occasion wasn't over as tea, sandwiches and cigars were produced and brandy flowed freely. Captain Fletcher was offered a snifter of brandy and a cigar, but he demurred as he and the general had a meeting back at the military headquarters. General Hamilton assured Byron there was no urgency and for a short time they joined the men in a drawing room which quickly filled with smoke and lively jocularity.

Still surprised and euphoric, Byron rode back with the general to his office at headquarters. When they entered his office a visitor was waiting. Next to his desk stood an attractive young woman. The general then introduced the young lady, "Captain, I would be remiss if I did not introduce you to my daughter, Lady Ellen. Her mother died some time back and she now lives here with me and assists

158

me on formal occasions." Byron acknowledged the young lady with a nod. Lady Ellen Hamilton smiled warmly, and with a curtsy departed.

"Now Captain, down to business," began the general, "Since I arrived here I have been understaffed. I have decided to select an aide-de-camp and I want you to fill that position. Although you are young, you have had battle experience and display management skills necessary for the position. Captain, this is not a request, it is an order."

For the second time in just hours Byron was nearly speechless. But an order from a general is an order obeyed.

"Sir, I accept with honor."

"I expected no less. Now, Captain, let's enjoy that cigar and a snifter of brandy."

Byron had not entirely comprehended the events of the day when he and Boaz boarded a vessel back to Auckland. Later he would have time to appreciate what had happened, but now, as senior officer, he still had command of Blandford base and was determined to hand it over to a new commander in fighting condition. General Hamilton gave him a month for transition to his new position as aide-de-camp. In addition the general wanted Captain Fletcher to make recommendations on how to deal with the Maori conflict, as the fighting so far had been less than successful. What could be done to defeat these fierce warriors?

For some time Byron had been interested in learning the Maori language. He believed it would be beneficial in his new responsibilities in Wellington so he asked young Matiu to be his teacher. Matiu was excited when asked since it meant he would follow his captain to Wellington.

When the Shillingstones' postmaster became aware of the contents of the envelope from the court of Queen Victoria addressed to Mr. Howard Fletcher, he sent a messenger to deliver it personally. He also sent a messenger to Sarah with a special note as well. Within hours the village of Shillingstone became aware that one of their own had receive the nation's highest military honor, the "Victoria Cross."

Sergeant Wilson was in his usual place at the Old Ox Inn when he received a letter from the Commander of Camp Aldershot. He was curious as he had never received a letter from Aldershot. What could it be? When he opened it he was surprised and pleased with what he read. As a retired soldier with the Bengal Horse Artillery he was informed that a previous officer of his acquaintance, Captain Byron Fletcher, had received the Victoria Cross for valor in the face of the enemy while fighting in New Zealand. Upon receiving this incredible news, Sergeant Wilson immediately told everyone he knew, even before ordering a pint to celebrate.

Sarah was pleased to receive a note about her beloved, but had no idea what it was about. When a neighbor came over to congratulate her on the news he explained the significance of the Victoria Cross. Sarah was even more pleased and very proud of the man who would return to marry her. Shillingstone was all abuzz about Byron for the rest of the day. It was rumored that the weekly newspaper would print a detailed story about one of their own receiving such an honor. This created more excitement in the village than a visit by the Prince of Wales.

Three weeks later Sarah received a letter from Byron letting her know that he was moving from his base in Auckland to a base in Wellington, the new capital of New Zealand. He was now an aide-de-camp to General Hamilton, commander of the army in New Zealand. He made no mention of receiving the Victoria Cross for valor in battle. He loved her and would write more later.

AIDE-DE-CAMP

Captain Fletcher, Matiu and Boaz arrived at their new assignment in Wellington and were allotted living quarters on the military base. As a mere farm boy from Shillingstone, Byron wondered if he was up to the duties to which he had been assigned. Then he reflected on what he had experienced in India, China and now New Zealand, and his doubts dissipated.

His new commander, Sir General Hamilton, had been successful in battle and in performing his administrative duties for Her Majesty Queen Victoria. New Zealand was a new colony in the British Empire and would be in worthy hands. He was the sole heir of his father's estate on six hundred acres outside Battlesbridge, Essex. While serving the Crown he had little time to spend at his estate. In Wellington he rented a residence befitting a man of his station, which was large enough to entertain politicians, diplomats and dignitaries with private quarters for himself and his daughter Ellen.

Challenges quickly piled up for Captain Fletcher. In the 1860s gold had been discovered on the South Island, at a place called Gabriel's Gully. Prospectors from California, Australia, and other parts of the world poured into the area. At one time there were more than 14,000 prospectors scrounging for gold on the South Island. Rumor had it that if a person just spat upon the ground there would be gold below. Law and order became the responsibility of the army under General Hamilton and Captain Fletcher. Officers of the Dragoon Light Horse Cavalry were sent to the South Island to administer law and order, which they did successfully.

Maori attacks and ambushes continued on the North Island. A group of 75 Maori warriors kept 3.000 Imperial soldiers engaged in fighting. Tactics by the English were ineffective, as hills and dense forests gave an advantage to the native Maori. Byron informed General Hamilton that the conflict would last for years, but at some point the natives would have to realize that they would have fewer warriors while the English would always have soldiers available.

Under a white flag, Captain Fletcher, Matiu and three cavalry officers traveled to many Maori communities. With Byron speaking in their native language, they were open to his message of a compromise with the settlers. While fighting continued, the Maori began to understand that they would never rid their country of English settlers nor the British colonial government.

General Hamilton was aware that Captain Fletcher exercised Boaz every morning. Accordingly, he asked the captain to include Lady Ellen on these morning rides. Lady Ellen's horse, Queen, had recently arrived from England and Ellen was anxious to have her exercised. Byron agreed to the general's request. He had thought Ellen was a pleasant young woman and viewed her like he would a sister.

When Lady Ellen arrived at the stables, Byron was in for a surprise. He had never seen a woman ride astride a horse like a man. She was attractive in her split-legged riding dress. Her horse was a beautiful German Brandenburger bay, a breed known for its even-tempered personality. Before they began their ride Lady Ellen introduced Queen to Byron and Boaz.

Like a gentleman, Byron offered to assist Lady Ellen in mounting her ride which she kindly declined and adroitly mounted Queen by herself. Lady Ellen was a skilled horsewoman and rode her mount as well as a cavalry officer. They trotted from the base and rode on trails over the hills and valleys that surrounded Wellington. Entering an open area, their horses seemed anxious to run. They started at a trot, went to a canter, and then to a full gallop. Grass, trees and splashing streams rapidly flew by. Byron could not remember having such an enjoyable ride. Back at base stable hands removed both saddles and tack, then washed and brushed the horses down before turning them out to pasture. Lady Ellen turned to Byron with a smile and announced, "I would like you to call me Ellen, and shall we ride tomorrow?" As often as they were able, Byron and Ellen rode around Wellington, talking, laughing, and racing one another. It became almost a daily routine.

While General Hamilton and his daughter lived in a large home, Captain Fletcher resided in rather modest officers' quarters. The general felt that in his new position Byron deserved better housing and asked Ellen if she minded if the captain had a suite in their residence. She looked at her father with a devilish smile and answered, "Well...all right." Byron accepted the offer if young Matiu could come as well. They agreed.

As time passed Byron no longer regarded Ellen like a sister. Nature had a way of getting entangled in a relationship between a handsome young man and a beautiful young woman. Encouraged by her father, they spent a lot of time together. New Zealand was an incredibly scenic country with valleys, forested mountains and spectacular waterfalls. They explored places of interest and took long trail rides in romantic settings. Something began to happen. Byron was both excited and scared. Was this possibly the beginning of a saddle romance? He feared it might be, yet he was still thinking about Sarah. After so many years away from her he wondered, had he really made a commitment for love, and was he now bound to his promise to marry Sarah?

For the past twelve years most of Byron's expressions of love for Sarah had been limited to letters. Her correspondence had been much the same. She was clearly unhappy and wished she had made a different decision. More than once he had wondered what would have happened if he had refused to wait for her. Would her decision have been different? Some time back, Byron had a dream that he and Sarah were sitting in front of her fireplace looking into the warmth of the fire, laughing and talking until the flames became embers. As the embers began to die down they talked in low whispers. After the fire was reduced to cold ashes, they sat silently for a long time and said nothing. When he awoke the next morning, he was troubled and wondered if there was any meaning to the dream.

On his last visit home there were several occasions when there seemed to be a hollow echo in their expressions of love. He loved Sarah, but now it wasn't the same. It was a promise, a commitment, a word of honor, a duty. He was trying to sort out his emotions while being true to himself and to Sarah. Many times he wondered if she would ever say yes without conditions. He finally came to the conclusion that she would always be bound by her family, and that she would never agree to marry him.

For years he had lived under the shadow of his father's opinion of women. In recent years Byron's views began to change. Ellen helped him to believe that men and women were neither above nor below one another. A bond of equality with Ellen had enabled Byron to be set free from the prison his father had placed him. However, Sarah had never been able to escape from the prison in which she allowed her father to place her. Neither the death of Christopher, nor the death of her mother released Sarah from the obligation of loyalty to her father. She still felt an obligation to care for him while he lived in their home. Byron had been set free; Sarah had not.

After many months traveling back and forth between Shillingstone and Shrewsbury, Sarah's father told Sarah he had met a widow named Sophia who had three young children. He had rented a room from her while surveying in and around Shrewsbury. In time he had fallen in love with her and she had agreed to marry him. With her three children, Sophia would become the wife and mother that Mildred had never been. When he told Sarah of his decision she was shocked and became angry. She felt cheated, betrayed and cast aside. He was the reason she had turned down Byron's proposal of marriage and now he would be gone. She would be alone. She felt like she had been pushed off a cliff and was falling with no bottom in sight.

During one of many sleepless nights she had a dream about a beautiful large apple tree in the middle of a fenced pasture in which resided a bull and his harem. The apples were bountiful and tasty. Unfortunately, local villagers could not collect any as the bull would not permit anyone in the pasture. All the apples fell rotting to the ground or were eaten by the cattle. Waking up the next morning she found the dream disturbing. What did it mean? Was Byron beyond her reach? As before, she wondered what her life would be like if she had married him. The dream left her feeling melancholy.

At least she knew that at some time in the next several years Byron would return, they would be married, and her life would be better. In the meantime she invited her Aunt Edith to share the cottage with her for moral and financial support.

Andy Clark, Klaus's apprentice, would often stop by to see if there was anything that needed to be fixed in the cottage. There was always something and she always offered Andy tea and conversation when he was finished. He brightened her day, and she thought of Andy as a nice, considerate young many

TWO LETTERS

During a dark cloudy night in November of 1869 two steamships passed each other in opposite directions midpoint on the Red Sea, south of the Suez Canal. One sailed south destined for New Zealand with a bag of letters including one addressed to Captain Byron Fletcher in Wellington, New Zealand. A north sailing ship destined for England carried bags of letters including a letter addressed to Sarah Glanville in the village of Shillingstone, Dorset, England.

My dear loving Byron:

Ever since you left, my life has been difficult and it feels like I'm falling apart. First young Christopher died, then my mother and now my father has left to marry a widow in Shrewsbury. These words from my father still ring in my ears, "Every father should have a wonderful daughter like you." For years I have been a prisoner to those words. Now I feel abandoned by him. I gave my life for my family, now I have no one. My Aunt Edith told me I would be making a mistake when I asked for more time to address my family needs. It was a mistake I regret greatly. I am willing to do anything I can do to right a wrong decision. I have always loved you and none other. Now I dream about the day we will be married in front of the vicar in our Church of the Holy Rood. Do you remember when you were home last and we went to church and sat silently in your pew looking at the altar where we would be married? Now that can become a reality. I love you and want to be your wife. I am free from any more family obligations or responsibilities. I love you more than ever. If you were here and asked me again to marry you I would say, "Yes, yes and yes!"

I pray you will be excited and receptive to this wonderful news. Let me know if you have any idea when you expect to return.

All my love and devotion, your darling Sarah

Dear Sarah,

It has been some time since I last wrote. I now write a letter I find difficult to put into words.

My father had a large influence on my view of women. He maintained that deference should always be paid to a member of the fairer sex. That played a part in my willingness to give you time to work out the challenges you had at home. I gave in to your wishes not once, but twice. Once in a while I have wondered what you would have done if I had decided not to wait to be married. Would your decision have been different? I have come to the realization that it would have been the same. When the choice came down to your family or me, I was the one rejected. You spurned my offer of marriage and the advice of your Aunt Edith.

In my years away from home I have traveled thousands of miles and have been to three continents. During this time I have been through battles and have seen all manner of bloodshed and death. All that time I have been faithful in my love for you in the hope of spending the rest of our lives together. That hope is lost.

When I was transferred to New Zealand I found a new life and a new love. I was introduced to Ellen Hamilton, the daughter of Sir Victor Hamilton, commander of the British army here in New Zealand. Over time Ellen and I have developed a mutual affection, and now wish to become husband and wife. By the time you receive this letter we will have been married in the Anglican Church in Wellington. When my assignment is finished here in New Zealand we look forward to making our home in Shillingstone.

I wish you the best, good health and the support of your family.

Byron

A MILITARY WEDDING

As a young lady of means growing up in Essex, Lady Ellen Hamilton had had numerous suitors, none of whom she found acceptable. When she arrived in New Zealand, finding a husband was not on her mind. Her thoughts moderated after an introduction to a handsome young red-haired Captain Byron Fletcher. She was impressed with his chivalry when they first rode together. After many such experiences, conversations and dinners at home, Ellen developed an emotional attachment to him. She was aware of the battles he had fought, yet he had not been sullied or tainted by the horrors of war. He had a mature accepting wholesomeness and a gracious, pleasant personality. The captain cut a muscular silhouette along with his beautiful rust-red hair. Dressed in formal military uniform, he was irresistible. There was no doubt she was in love with Byron and wanted him for her husband.

Living in General Hamilton's home with his daughter gave Byron the opportunity to know Ellen, a beautiful, elegant young woman. She was poised, statuesque and graceful. As they rode together almost daily, he grew to recognize her confidence, independence and energy. Byron became enthralled with her. Now at age thirty-three, love found him anew. But this time it was a mature love without conditions. She was a lady of nobility and he was a farm boy from a small hamlet. It made no difference. They were not children, they were a mature man and woman who were deeply in love. After an appropriate period of courtship, and with the full approval of Ellen's father, Byron asked Ellen to marry him and she readily agreed.

In every frontier city there were two buildings of importance, a government house and a church. The city of Wellington had both. Saint Paul's Anglican Church was built with native wood by eight skilled carpenters and was completed in the summer of 1866. It was in this church, in 1869, that Captain Byron Fletcher and Lady Ellen Grace Hamilton were to be married.

Their wedding was the social event of the season in Wellington. With a population of almost 7,000, almost everyone knew of General Hamilton and knew that his daughter was about to marry Captain Fletcher.

In preparation for this wedding Saint Paul's had been beautifully decorated in New Zealand's dazzling fall colors. Each side of the communion table had several bouquets of flowers and a large ceremonial candle stood to the right of the table.

By mid-morning friends, politicians, military officers, dignitaries plus Wellington's citizens filled Saint Paul's to witness the wedding ceremony performed by Bishop Charles Abraham. Byron stood at the altar in his formal officer's uniform, while General Hamilton wore his full dress uniform and medals. Ellen's bridal dress was a striking white empire silhouette with veil and train. To strains of "The Wedding March" General Hamilton slowly walked down the aisle with his Ellen on his arm. As they approached Bishop Abraham, General Hamilton gave Lady Ellen's hand to

Captain Fletcher, which was happily accepted. The couple then turned and faced the bishop to recite their vows.

In full liturgical robes, Bishop Abraham proceeded with the wedding ceremony, including vows, prayers, a homily on marriage, and the exchange of rings. He concluded with a blessing, "Now that Byron and Ellen have given themselves to each other by solemn vows, with the joining of hands and the giving and receiving of rings, I pronounce that they are husband and wife. In the name of the Father, and of the Son and of the Holy Ghost." They sealed their vows with a kiss, and smiling, turned to the congregation to be presented as husband and wife. With the organ playing a recessional they exited the church under an arch of sabers held by Captain Fletcher's cavalry officers.

Guest enjoyed a morning brunch at Government House hosted by Governor Grey. It was similar to a banquet with champagne, a variety of wines, and Earl Grey tea. A centerpiece on the table was a three-tiered wedding fruit cake decorated with beautiful white frosting. Byron and Ellen made the first slice with a sword, and with joined hands on the hilt, cut into the cake with the tip of the sword.

Invitees were entertainment by a string ensemble as they visited and congratulated the newly-married couple. Captain and Lady Ellen would have a honeymoon in several weeks, with the destination to be announced later. As the afternoon wore on, the newlyweds bade their guest's farewell and they retired to their private residence in General Hamilton's home.

THE LETTER

It was an unusually warm autumn day in Shillingstone. Leaves had turned a variety of red, yellow and brown along the banks of the River Stour. A neighbor told Sarah there was a letter for her at the post office. After months of not hearing from Byron it had to be from him. Sarah hurried to the post office and in her excitement said, "Mr. Chamberlin I have been told there is a letter for me. Is it from Byron?"

"Gracious me it is, and I was going to have someone fetch you to let you know, and here it is." Sarah was excited to get his letter but decided to wait and read it at home. She could hardly wait for what Byron had to say about her father leaving and that they could now be married.

It was a short letter. As she read she became puzzled. What was he trying to say? Reading the words, over and over, she felt like a mountain was about to fall on her. *Hope is lost! Did he not read my letter? Maybe it got lost or had not yet reached him. How could he say this?* She put the letter on her lap, unable to read further. She was beyond shock! Moisture in her eyes changed into a torrent of tears. She sobbed, shaking uncontrollably. *Why, why?* His letter slipped off her lap to the floor. She rocked back and forth moaning with deep guttural sounds from the depth of her soul.

How long she remained that way she didn't know. At last she lifted her head and took a deep breath. She bent over and picked up the letter and through moist eyes tried to finish reading it. They were words she didn't want to understand, and sobbing, she went to bed.

The neighbor who told Sarah about the letter also passed the news to her Aunt Edith who was at the market that day. Edith surmised it must be from Byron, because she knew Sarah was anxious to hear from him in response to her letter. When Edith came home to their cottage the door was slightly ajar and all she could hear was moaning. She saw Sarah curled up on her bed with knees bent and arms clutched around her stomach. Sarah was oblivious to her aunt's presence. A letter on the floor caught Edith's attention. She picked it up and read it through moist eyes and understood Sarah's grief. Edith prepared some hot water for tea. She sat beside Sarah, rubbing her back for comfort.

Time was lost as the sun slid below the horizon. Edith lit candles and finally Sarah uncurled her body, stretched out her legs and sat on the side of her bed staring at the floor. No words were spoken. Edith gave her a cup of tea, which Sarah accepted and sipped between sobs. Neither knew what to do so they sat in silence. Edith finally stoked the fireplace for light and warmth. They had another cup of tea. After several hours both were emotionally and physically exhausted. Edith lay beside Sarah and pulled a blanket over both of them. Sleep finally came.

The following morning an autumn sun was not to be found, only low clouds and misting drizzle. Slowly Edith and Sarah began to move and stretch their limbs. Edith wanted to help and Sarah tried to pull herself together. Over tea and buttered bread, life slowly returned to Sarah. Edith confirmed that she had read Byron's letter and was shocked at what he had said. Did he mean what he wrote? Byron was now beyond Sarah's reach both in distance and in marriage. She strode over and looked out her old window and only saw misty clouds and cold rain. She was devastated.

In a small hamlet like Shillingstone, good news travels as fast as a clap of thunder, bad news faster. In recent years Sarah had lost her brother and her mother, had been left by her father, and now had been abandoned by the one she was to marry. Only Sarah and Edith knew the reason why. During the morning hours Sarah admitted to herself that she had made the wrong decision and now must live with the result. It was hard to admit, even more difficult to accept. She didn't want to leave her cottage or face anyone in the village. Would she ever get over losing Byron?

A most unlikely sympathetic person was the apprentice blacksmith, Andy Clark. Every day he saw Sarah make her trips to the post office and would often take a moment to chat. He had seen her the previous day when she bounced out of the post office with the excitement of a little girl. Later he could not believe the rumors about Sarah losing the man she was to marry. He wished there was something he could do in her difficult circumstances. He remembered his own grim life before becoming a blacksmith.

For generations Andy's family had been farm laborers. They were the poorest of the poor, receiving little pay and uncertain work. By his eighteenth birthday Andy realized there was no future in farm labor and decided to try something else. He sought work with the chimney sweep, the thatcher, the boot maker, the carpenter and the village mason. None had any interest in him and turned him away. Last on his list was the village blacksmith. Andy approached Klaus and interrupted his work, asking him if he needed any help.

Klaus paused, looked him up and down, and asked, "Vot can u do?"

Andy replied, "I haven't been taught to read or write, but I'm good with numbers."

Klaus gave him some numbers to add and subtract. He answered quickly and correctly. "Boy, u dun vell, I vant u back, ve talk."

Andy quickly answered, "Yes, yes, I'll be back."

Unknown to Andy, Klaus and his wife Helga, had been thinking about returning to their home in Austria. They'd had a good life in Shillingstone, but as they became older they felt the call of their homeland and a desire to be with their family. Perhaps this young man could learn the blacksmithing trade. Helga asked her husband about Andy and what he looked like. Klaus told her he was of good stature, strong from farm work, good with numbers and appeared to have an agreeable personality. Andy's decision to talk to Klaus showed initiative and drive.

When Andy returned, Klaus told him he would take him on as an apprentice for a month to evaluate his ability to become a smithy. By the end of that month, Andy was being treated like the son that Klaus wished he'd had. He was a quick learner, motivated for perfection and delighted to be under Klaus's supervision. Helga took an instant delight in having such a young man working with her husband. After work, Andy often went home with Klaus and enjoyed Helga's cooking. He had never eaten so well nor had he felt so appreciated in all his young life.

About this time other events were occurring in Shillingstone. In November of 1868, a violent storm from the east swept through the village and the 86-foot Maypole came crashing down. While there was some initial disappointment, interest in the annual festival had diminished. It was uncertain whether there would be another Maypole erected. After the railway came, the world had expanded and there were many other opportunities for travel and entertainment in other communities. Traditions of previous generations began to fade.

After all her work in reviving interest in the Maypole Festival, Gertrude Haggardy was saddened by the pole's demise. As she grew older and heavier she had little energy to do anything more for the festival. Since she had accomplished her goal of becoming a queen bee it was time to retire, as her health had declined. Much of her days were spent in bed, her only exercise, eating.

There had been a rumor circulating that the village blacksmith was thinking of returning to Austria. After six years of working with Klaus, Andy Clark became a skilled blacksmith. He had learned the craft and was almost equal to

Klaus. However, Andy would never be able to lift Mrs. Sour's six-hundred-pound pig.

At 24 years of age Andy was a prime target for mothers with unmarried daughters. He was secure in his craft and was earning a good income. Andy was good-looking, in great physical condition and was a likable person. With a ratio of one eligible man for five or more unmarried maidens, Andy had choices for a wife. He wanted to marry, but none of the young ladies in the village interested him. There was only one woman in his thoughts. She was nine years his senior and her name was Sarah.

A HONEYMOON TO REMEMBER

Several weeks after their wedding Byron and Ellen took an extended honeymoon to the South Island of New Zealand. They had never been there and Byron felt it would also be an opportunity to tour the island in his position as aide-de-camp. Their destination was the beautiful city of Christchurch, several hundred nautical miles south of Wellington. Sailing on a coastal steamer for two days they approached Pegasus Harbor. Standing on the ship's deck, they had a stunning view that lay before them. The city was situated on the shore of a large curved harbor whose land slowly rose up to a landscape of tall mountains. With a blue sky above and calm blue waters below, the harbor displayed a stunning panorama of towering trees pointing up to snowcapped mountains. Their view in this marvelous romantic place portended a wonderful life together.

While in Christchurch Byron and Ellen were guests of Reverend Henry James, Vicar of Christchurch Cathedral. A comfortable guest suite in the church rectory was provided for the newlyweds. Their honeymoon was off to a great beginning. Over the next several days, Reverend James gave them a tour of the city and surrounding area. He suggested it was possible that the name of the city came from Christchurch in Dorset, the area where Byron had been born. Both were impressed with the newness, the size and the beauty of the city's buildings.

After a week there they sailed 250 miles south to tour gold fields recently discovered in Gabriel's Gulch. For over three days they navigated down the east coast of South Island and anchored in the harbor of Dunedin. The contrast between Christchurch and Dunedin could not have been more dramatic. Dunedin was dirty, scruffy and overcrowded. Thousands of men and women from around the world had tramped through this frontier town hoping to find gold in Gabriel's Gulch. Most failed and departed, leaving litter everywhere.

Their host in Dunedin was Reverend Dr. Donald M. Stuart, first minister of Knox Church. Dr. Stuart was a genial host and somewhat self-conscious at the modest housing of the church rectory in Dunedin, compared to the one in Christchurch. Byron had previously experienced many primitive situations and regardless found their accommodations satisfactory. After a day's rest, Dr. Stuart arranged for a carriage tour to the gold fields, guided by a retired miner. After several miles they arrived at Tuapeka, a small river that slowly wound through a shallow gully. Tents and shacks of all descriptions were perched on each hillside. An odious smell and dense smoke settled low in the valley as miners worked the rock-strewn shore of Gabriel's Gulch. Hundreds of men and a few women crawled over the river banks like an army of ants, all seeking their fortune in gold. Few were successful. Byron and Ellen spent little time at the foul smelling site and returned to Dunedin.

Prior to sailing north back to Christchurch, Captain Fletcher decided to sail to the most southern tip of the island, some 150 miles distant. Ellen, a plucky traveler, wanted to see everything with her new husband. When they entered the Port of Bluff it looked like other port in New Zealand with beautiful scenery and dotted with numerous small islands. Beautiful mountains were covered with a blanket of trees, and a gigantic glacier calving at the water's edge. On shore the district superintendent offered a carriage tour of the area. Neither Byron nor Ellen had ever seen such a mammoth glacier up close and they were transfixed, watching the glacier calving large chucks of ice into the bay. After their tour of Port of Bluff, they returned to their ship and sailed back toward Christchurch.

After sailing north, at times in rough seas, they were thankful when Pegasus Bay came into view. Soon they were moored at Christchurch Harbor, eager for several days' rest in the comfortable guest suite in the church rectory. Their genial hosts, the Reverend James and his wife, were pleased that they had returned safely. Reverend James inquired, "What do you think of the rest of the South Island?"

Byron responded, "It is beautiful in its forests, mountains and glaciers. Most of it is virgin territory, wild and untamed. Some day that will change."

They settled into their suite and looked forward to a good night's rest.

During the night in late November, 1869, an earthquake suddenly struck the city of Christchurch. The earth vibrated and buildings swayed causing some of them to collapse with thunderous grinding sounds and thick clouds of dust. Byron and Ellen were asleep in the guest suite when a top section of the church spire came crashing down on the roof of the rectory. Debris from the spire fell on the area over the guest suite, smashing through the roof and landing on Byron and Ellen. A layer of dust covered them like a gray blanket. Awakened by the earthquake, the church sexton lit a lantern and rushed upstairs to check on the guests. Brushing aside debris, he entered the suite and with the light of his lantern saw a large hole in the roof, and rubble spread across the floor. In his dim light he saw the dust-covered body of Captain Fletcher sheltering his wife. He lay unmoving, like a gray toppled statue, as Mrs. Fletcher lay on her back with her right arm extended. There was no movement. With such little light the sexton believed he was looking at two lifeless bodies.

Straightaway he found Reverend James and told him what he had seen. Confusion reigned. The sexton was ordered to get more men and more lanterns for the suite. A servant was directed to send a telegram to Governor Grey in Wellington to inform him of the earthquake and also to announce the deaths of the captain and Mrs. Fletcher.

As darkness gave way to the gray of an early morning, five men stood transfixed by the large hole in the ceiling of the rectory. Dust, bricks, stone and chunks from the church spire lay on the floor. While they were pondering what to do, they heard a quiet moan and noticed Ellen's right arm give a slight twitch. She was not dead. One of the men informed the pastor who immediately called for a doctor. They then moved Byron and discovered that although he was unconscious, he was still breathing.

By the time the doctor arrived Lady Ellen was moaning loudly. The doctor immediately asked for a pail of warm water, clean rags and clean blankets. Taking charge, he had the Fletchers moved to the next bedroom which had not been damaged. He checked Captain Fletcher's breathing and found it satisfactory. The pastor's wife washed the dust from Lady Ellen's eyes, ears, nose and mouth. The doctor cleaned a wound on Captain Fletcher's head and found to his great relief that it was not critical.

Before the doctor left, Byron awoke but had no memory of what had happened. For a week both would be sore, bruised and uncomfortable, but they were survivors of the earthquake of 1869.

Early issues of local Wellington newspapers ran articles about the magnitude of the earthquake in Christchurch and reported the death of the newlywed couple. It was not until late afternoon that it was announced that the couple had not died. After recuperating for a week, Byron and Ellen returned to Wellington. It would be another month before they would fully recover.

DEATH OF A MATRIARCH

After months of declining health, Mrs. Gertrude Haggardy died, presumably from heart failure. She was greatly appreciated by the wives of Shillingstone, as Gertrude had opened the door which enabled them to enjoy some of the social graces of the gentry. It was her introduction of afternoon tea that provided an opportunity for the village women to socialize among themselves.

She seldom left her home. Instead, villagers came to her residence to visit, to ask for advice and to request assistance in dire circumstances. Gertrude's door was open to anyone in Shillingstone. Most who sought her out were the working men and women. She was a matriarchal symbol of the community and she believed she was the queen bee of her domain.

In anticipation of her death Gertrude Haggardy had given instructions to Reverend Dayman concerning her funeral and interment. Shillingstone was her home and she wished for a funeral in the Church of the Holy Rood, and to be buried in the church cemetery. While she had lived her life with panache, she wished a simple service and a statement of appreciation to the people of the village for their acceptance and support for her as a member of their community.

She gave Reverend Dayman legal authority to sell her residence on Church Street and to donate the proceeds for the development of a community park. Thankfully she did not wish a monument as it would likely be substantial.

On the day of Gertrude's funeral, the Church of the Holy Rood was filled with working class villagers in recognition of her contribution to their lives. The minister gave an appropriate homily and then moved to the cemetery for her burial. Only a group like blacksmiths Klaus Oberdorf, Andy Clark and six other large men were able to carry Gertrude's casket to her gravesite. After an appropriate observance for the dead, Reverend Dayman declared, "We therefore commit her body to the ground; earth to earth, ashes to ashes and dust to dust; in sure and certain hope of the Resurrection and eternal life. Amen." Mourners then moved to the rectory for refreshments, prepaid by Gertrude.

Sarah and her Aunt Edith were part of the gathering remembering Gertrude. When the service concluded they walked back home to Sarah's cottage. With the combination of Edith's rent and the sale of Sarah's spun wool they would be able to survive financially. Sarah began to feel a little better over her grief of losing Byron.

Edith wondered if Sarah was aware of a young man who had taken an interest in her. Andy, the blacksmith, was always thinking of excuses to visit Sarah. One day he noticed her dirty old window, with myriad bubbles and wavy glass. He offered to replace it, but Sarah demurred, explaining, "I would like to keep it just as it is." For Sarah, Andy was no more than a nice young man who worked with Klaus at the forge, but Edith suggested otherwise. In response Sarah joked that she was an old spinster, much too old for a young man like Andy. Edith was concerned that her niece was still emotionally tied to Byron.

One afternoon Sarah asked Edith to visit Sergeant Wilson at the Old Ox Inn and ask if he had heard anything from Byron. As a widow, Edith was reluctant to enter an inn alone, but she agreed to talk to the sergeant. Wilson had no information about Byron, but surprisingly asked if she would stay to visit and have a pint with him. Edith surprised herself and agreed.

ADJUTANT OFFICER

While Byron and Ellen were in the South Island, General Hamilton's adjutant officer had been recalled to England and was assigned to deal with discord in Africa during the Boer conflict. When the Fletchers returned to Wellington from the earthquake and had time to recover, General Hamilton decided to appoint Byron as his new Adjutant Officer. "Captain, you have been successful as my aide-de-camp, but now I need you as an Adjutant Officer of the army in New Zealand. In truth you will be the person who is second in command. I am also promoting you to the grade of major, appropriate for the responsibility of such a position. You have traveled to most points on the North Island and have communicated with hundreds of Maori leaders. Your understanding of the relationship among the Maori, the settlers, and the government was paramount to this promotion. We have been fighting with the Maori for thirty years and the British government wants this conflict settled."

Byron responded, "Sir, I am honored by the promotion to major and your confidence in my ability to fulfill the responsibility as Adjutant Officer. I will review the current situation with the Maori and recommend appropriate measures to deal with this conflict."

"Major, I expected nothing less."

From his experience in India and China, Byron concluded that historically, wars were often decided by a single battle or, over time, by wearing an enemy down. He believed there

189

would be no conclusive battle with the Maori. They were made up of many tribes scattered in the hills and valleys of New Zealand. A solution would come when the Maori realized that eventually their population would become smaller as the opposition grew larger. When settlers first arrived in New Zealand in 1840 the Maori outnumbered the settlers by forty to one. By 1870 it was reversed as the colonials and Europeans exceeded the Maori by four to one. Isolated fighting would continue, but within a few years they would lose their bargaining power.

Missionaries in New Zealand had a positive influence on the Maori culture. They translated the native language into written words and converts were required to reject their barbaric practices. While there was never a large Christian population among the Maori, converts were like yeast in a loaf of bread.

Instead of a large army, Major Fletcher recommended using fewer soldiers. He decided on a ratio of five soldiers to every Maori warrior. British soldiers were then trained in guerilla warfare and were to become familiar with the environment in which they would fight. With these factors taken into consideration, Byron believed the Maori fighting would eventually be under control. He predicted that peace would be restored by the end of 1871.

After reviewing this information, General Hamilton accepted the recommendations and declared, "Now, Major, get the job done!"

Young Matiu was now living on the Blandford base and would play an important part in Major Fletcher's plan. A dozen teams with six cavalry officers each were to travel the length and width of the North Island to communicate a clear message about the benefits of peace. One member of every team was required to speak the Maori language and Matiu agreed to undertake this task as speaking Maori showed respect and improved communication.

Sir George Ferguson Bowen had recently been appointed governor of New Zealand, and was determined to reconcile the Maori with British rule. He had been successful as governor in Queensland, Australia, and approved of Major Fletcher's campaign.

Byron seldom traveled as he was an essential part of the headquarters as the adjutant officer. He worked closely with General Hamilton, Governor Bowen, political and business leaders, all committed to helping bring peace to both islands.

Living close to home in Wellington, Byron was pleased to spend more time with his new bride. Her father was as delighted with her choice of a husband as was Ellen. As often as possible they rode their horses around the countryside of Wellington just as they had in their earlier acquaintance. At times their conversation turned to where they might live when they returned to England. Byron's term of service concluded at the end of 1871 and Shillingstone was dear to his heart. Would Ellen find a small village acceptable after having a large "manor house" back in Essex? Only two options were considered, Shillingstone or her father's "manor house". First Byron had to be mustered out of the army in Camp Aldershot. A decision on their residence would be made later.

Over the ensuing year, progress with the Maori became evident. Fighting decreased and the Maori leadership came to understand that working with the British was their best option for a future in their homeland. Their warrior aggression would no longer succeed on the battlefield, but would always be a part of their culture.

Major Fletcher's leadership as adjutant, and his role in bringing about peace were recognized by General Hamilton and Governor Bowen. A special retirement reception was held in the large ballroom at Government House. Byron was praised for his insight and persistence in dealing with the Maori problem. He received a Medal of Merit for his service in the British Dragoon Light Horse Cavalry and also for his service to the colony of New Zealand.

LAST CHANCE

Seven years after the arrival of the Dorset Central Railway there were many changes in Shillingstone. New horizons were open for travel across Dorset and all of England. The railway station had become the center of life for the village. However rail service did little to increase the population. Few had come and few had left. In 1800, Shillingstone had a population of 380, and by 1870 slightly over 500. The quality of life had improved, but had little impact on the village population.

Not everyone felt that life was better. Sarah had not accepted that Byron had a wife and was not coming back to marry her. She still loved him, and as time went by her feelings continued to be strong. Every time she walked by the post office Sarah thought about Byron and wondered if there might be a different letter from him. None came.

Her Aunt Edith was in a quandary about what to do with her. Sarah was despondent, making life miserable for them both. Andy Clark was clearly besotted with her. Why would Sarah ever consider marriage to a village blacksmith when she had been betrothed to Byron Fletcher, a war hero and an officer in the British Army? It was unthinkable.

While Sarah struggled with her emotions, Byron's father was quiet about information regarding his son. Howard was enormously proud of what Byron had accomplished in his service to the Crown with the British Army. While he didn't fully understand his son's marriage to Ellen, he accepted

Byron's decision and would wait for them to arrive home. While Byron had been away, work on the farm had become increasingly difficult. Howard finally hired a farmhand for the manual labor. It was his hope that one day his son would return and manage the farm and possibly expand it, but in his heart he knew that would never happen.

For Edith, hope was not lost. She would do anything possible to help Sarah get over her emotional distress and find a husband, but her hope collided with reality. Most Older men were married and young men were either married, or soon to be married. One candidate had potential, but Sarah showed little interest. For many marriage to a blacksmith was seen to be advantageous as it was one of the most essential trades in a village. There was a saying, "If you can't marry into nobility the next best option was to marry a blacksmith." Aware that Andy Clark was interested in Sarah, Edith set out to make a connection, but needed help.

She decided to ask Sergeant Wilson for his help as they had become close friends. She had cajoled him out of the Old Ox Inn and he had agreed to walk with her on trails around the village. They even shared a train ride to Blandford Forum to shop and have lunch. Edith had long been a widow, and Sergeant Wilson had never married. Working to help Sarah find a husband might have an interesting outcome for them both.

Edith asked the sergeant to visit Andy Clark and to ask him if he had any interest in Sarah. Reluctantly he agreed. His previous experience had been cussing out army trainees, but this was a request of a very different nature. If it wasn't Edith asking, he would have said no.

Several days later Sergeant Wilson stopped by Andy's shop and waited for an opening.

"Andy, I'm Sergeant Wilson, a friend of Miss Sarah Glanville's aunt, Edith Somersby." He continued, "You live at the Inn…that so?"

"'Tis so. You said something about Sarah?"

"Andy, I'm not good at this. Mrs. Somersby wants to know if you are…sweet on Sarah. She wants Sarah to be happy."

With dirty, sweaty hands Andy rubbed the back of his neck and appeared to be thinking. "Well…I like her…but I don't think she likes me."

"Andy, I don't know…but could Mrs. Somersby come by and talk to you about Sarah?"

"No harm if she does."

With his assignment complete, Sergeant Wilson later met Edith and reported that Andy would be willing for her to stop and talk about Sarah. Over the next two months Edith conspired to play matchmaker for the pair. Edith included Sarah and Andy when she and Sergeant Wilson went for Sunday walks along Shillingstone's charming pathways. Sarah seemed to warm up to Andy. After six months Edith thought romantic feelings between them might be great enough for Andy to propose.

Andy and Sarah were invited to join Edith and the sergeant for an intimate dinner at the Old Ox Inn. After finishing their meal, She and the sergeant made an excuse to leave, but would return. Andy knew this was his opening and timidly began, "Sarah, from the first day I saw you I was in love. I love you and want to marry you and be your husband. I will provide for you for the rest of your life. If you accept me, I would be the happiest man in Shillingstone."

Sarah was surprised and took a few minutes to think about what to say. She was respectful and replied, "Andy, this was a surprise but, I thank you for asking. I need a little time to think about your proposal. Would you give me a couple of days to think about it before I answer?" It was how she responded to a previous offer of marriage with disastrous results.

Andy was happy she didn't turn him down. He stammered, "Yes...Yes, I can wait."

Two days later Sarah came by his shop and thanked him for his proposal, but for personal reasons she could not accept his offer of marriage. Andy was confused and disappointed. There was nothing he could do to change her mind. They went their separate ways.

Edith was annoyed that Sarah had refused Andy. There was nothing more she could do. Apparently if Sarah could not have Byron, she didn't want anyone. Over the next two months both women tried to come to terms with the trauma of Byron's letter. Or did they?

One day Edith came home to their little cottage and made a surprising announcement. Sergeant Wilson had asked her to marry him, and Edith had said yes. Edith said two mature adults who enjoyed time with each other decided to spend the rest of their lives together. Sarah had not seen it coming. She knew her aunt and Sergeant Wilson liked each other, but marriage?

"Are you really going to marry him?" Sarah implored.

"Yes."

"What am I going to do when you leave?" She asked in a sad choking voice.

"Sarah, you have had two offers of marriage and have turned down both. What did you expect would happen? Now you need to take care of yourself."

Sarah realized she would now be all alone. Finally with little conviction she said, "Andy is nice. I like him." After a pause she continued, "Well…if he asked me again, I would say yes."

"It's too late. A mother with a young daughter has been after Andy for several years and they were married two weeks ago."

Sarah was too focused on her own needs to be aware Andy had married. When informed of his marriage to some else she cried out, "What am I going to do?"

Sarah began to have the same feeling in her stomach as when she had read Byron's letter many times over. Words hit her again like a blacksmith's hammer on the anvil of her mind. "Hope is lost." Everyone had abandoned her. She wanted to hide in her bed forever.

COMING HOME

In anticipation of their return home, Major Fletcher sent a telegram to Reverend Dayman, vicar of the Church of the Holy Rood, to inquire about available housing for himself and his new bride. Two months later a letter from the vicar arrived and he indicated that the former home of Mrs. Haggardy was for sale. It was a large five bedroom house and was fully furnished. With no interest to date there was still a possibility it could be rented. Byron was familiar with the house on Church Road and believed it would suit them well.

Ellen had been born in the Hamilton Manor home on a six-hundred-acre estate in Essex. She was a child when her mother died and she had no memory of her or of the home. In the following years she had accompanied her father on his appointments as a British officer. She had never really lived on the estate as a child. In contrast, she realized the passion Byron felt for his home in Shillingstone. He often shared stories of growing up on his father's farm, planting and harvesting crops. It was his wish to return to his home, so with understanding and her love for Byron, Ellen agreed that they would initially establish a home in Shillingstone.

In late 1871 Byron's second enlistment with the British Army was about to expire. He looked forward to becoming a civilian once more. He first had to report to the base commander in Camp Aldershot to be mustered out of the army. When this was accomplished he and Ellen would be free to travel as they wished.

Fortunately, a navy flagship, the HMS Iron Duke, were returning from China bound for England with a stop in Wellington. In a coincidence, both ship and city had been named after the Duke of Wellington who had defeated Napoleon at the battle of Waterloo and there acquired the moniker of the Iron Duke. She was a newer iron-clad vessel launched in 1870 and was designed for overseas service. For armament, she carried 20 muzzle-loading cannon and had a complement of four hundred sailors and officers. HMS Iron Duke was an impressive ship as she plied the waters of the Orient.

Preparations to leave New Zealand was more work than anticipated. Most of Byron's belongings were tightly packed in a single trunk, while Ellen's required six. All the tack for their two horses took a full crate as Boaz and Queen were to accompany them on the journey to England. With all Major Fletcher's duties settled, they awaited the arrival of the HMS Iron Duke. Upon arrival in Wellington, her beauty created quite a stir in port. Major Byron and Lady Ellen were assigned a well-appointed berth in the officers' quarters. The ship's captain and crew welcomed them aboard, and they were feted during the entire cruise. HMS Iron Duke departed Wellington Harbor during the last week of January, and, depending on sea conditions anticipated a sailing time of six weeks. Traveling through the Suez Canal shortened the distance considerably. For Byron and Ellen the voyage home was like a holiday with few responsibilities.

Within sight of land the couple excitedly embraced each other on the upper deck. They scanned the distance and saw a distant speck on the horizon that would be their home. Within a day the ship was tethered to the Naval Dock in Portsmouth. The Fletchers' luggage and horses were shipped by rail to the station in Shillingstone. Byron and Ellen then took a train to the Army camp in Aldershot.

Major Fletcher was disappointed to learn that General Pennefather had recently died and that General Daniel Lysons, whose experience was that of a quartermaster, was now base commander. On meeting him, Byron was less than impressed. In a dutiful manner, typical of a Quartermaster, General Lyons asked Byron to sign all the retired documents confirming that he was no longer a soldier in the Queen's army. He was now a civilian.

Prior to travelling to Shillingstone, Ellen wanted to visit her father's estate. Fortunately there was train service to London and then on to the village of Battelsbridge. No one had lived in the manor home for a long time, however, it was managed by an estate steward, Harold Gibbins. He and his wife Gladys, were the only servants living in the manor house as all the others had small cottages scattered around the estate.

Mr. Gibbins was surprised when Lady Ellen's carriage arrived at the estate. He greeted her warmly and was pleased to meet her husband, Major Fletcher. He asked his wife to prepare a room and to plan supper for the evening. Walking around the large manor, Ellen had mixed emotions. Every room was big, dark, and musty. All the furniture was draped with dust covers, including paintings on the walls. Entry to the manor led to an impressive foyer and then on to a sizable parlor with a fireplace. Byron followed Ellen to a large family library, a music room and a spacious formal dining room. With few exceptions all the windows were covered with heavy dark drapes. They decided not to ascend the grand staircase which led to the bedrooms as they would later go up when it was time to retire for the evening. Byron felt like he was walking through a large dark cave. He wondered how anyone could afford such a large home and estate.

After breakfast they took a carriage to the station in Battelsbridge for the trip to London and then on to Shillingstone. During the ride Byron asked Ellen how she felt about her stay in her old home. After some thought she admitted, "It felt strange and unwelcoming." She continued, "I cannot visualize us living comfortably in such a large home." Byron agreed.

At the main station in London they changed trains for Shillingstone. Byron was apprehensive. He had faced cannon fire, musket shot and enemy soldiers, but was not sure what he would face at the station. Ellen tried to calm his fears and was excited to see his village for the first time. Byron wanted to arrive quietly and take a carriage to his father's farm. Not a chance!

From the time Byron and Ellen arrived at Camp Aldershot, telegrams kept the Shillingstone Parish Council up to date on their progress. Union Jack flags and banners were draped about the station. A brass band had arrived from Sturminster Newton and played martial music thirty minutes prior to the train's arrival. It seemed half the village filled the long station platform. Excitement mounted as the engine's whistle split the air along with a ringing brass bell. As the train slowed, Byron looked out the window and was aghast at the sight on the platform. He was nervous getting off the train, so Ellen took charge and led him down the steps of the rail car to the sound of a brass band and shouts from a crowd of hundreds. The Parish Council members welcomed Byron home with his new bride. It seemed the shouting would never end. It finished when the band stopped playing. Byron was overwhelmed. He never expected such a welcome, nor did he feel he deserved it. After much backslapping and handshaking, Byron and Ellen finally reached their carriage which took them down Blandford Road to his father's farm. The silence on the farm was as overwhelming as the shouting crowd had been. Byron could not believe he was home.

Byron introduced the love of his life to his father. Howard would ordinarily shake a woman's hand, instead he put his arms around her, and embraced her, adding a kiss on the cheek. Her smile won his heart. Byron enjoyed a beer and Ellen a cup of tea. Then they went and checked on Boaz and Queen. As they neared the pasture, both horses sensed their approach and raced across the pasture like spring colts. All the members of their family were finally together again.

After dinner, with a fire crackling in the hearth, Howard lit up his clay pipe, sipped some homemade wine and soaked in the presence of his son and daughter-in-law. They planned to stay at the farm for a few days and inspect Gertrude's house on Church Road. They slept in Byron's boyhood bedroom. It was small and cozy. Who knew what might happen in such intimate quarters?

The following morning Byron and Ellen stopped at the church rectory to meet Reverend Dayman. He was relieved that Byron was home safely and was also pleased to meet Ellen. He knew the purpose of their visit and told them that the house was open. As they walked from the rectory down Church Road to Gertrude's place, the first thing they noticed was its charming appearance. When they walked through the front doorway, Ellen was immediately impressed by Gertrude's good taste in furniture and décor. Her home was well maintained and had everything Ellen wanted: a big drawing room, a large dining room, a library, a music room, and five bedrooms. They spent much of the day walking through the house and strolling around the grounds. Ellen was confident they could live there in comfort. Back at the rectory Byron met with the vicar and arranged to rent the house with the possibility of a later purchase. Ellen loved the house, and appreciated all that Gertrude had done.

On the way back to the farm Byron decided on a quick stop at the Old Ox Inn to chat with his old friend Sergeant Wilson, but the man was not to be found. He checked with the proprietor and was informed that the sergeant was married and was renting a cottage a short distance down Blandford Road. After receiving directions they found the small cottage. Byron knocked on the door and was speechless when it was opened by Sarah's Aunt Edith. Then Sergeant Wilson came up behind her and invited them in. What a pleasant surprise! Their visit was short, as Byron and Ellen needed to get their baggage from the train station and move into their new home. Edith invited them to stop by later when they were settled and Ellen said they would be pleased to do so.

On the way back to the farm, Byron told Ellen that Edith was Sarah's aunt and that he was surprised that she and Sergeant Wilson were married. Ellen thought it was wonderful that Edith and the sergeant were married. During the short trip to the farm Ellen quietly felt sorry for Sarah.

After a month they were well settled in Gertrude's house and Byron was able to walk around without creating a crowd. He also felt a need to change the name of their home. Once known as Haggardy's House, Ellen decided it should be called Hamilton House. Byron became known as The Major, while Lady Ellen preferred to be simply called Ellen, the major's wife.

A short distance away, Sarah still struggled with the loss of Byron. She was trying to make sense of all that had happened to her, but lack of sleep and little nourishment contributed to her emotional instability. She wondered if she was becoming like her mother when she would be overtaken with exhaustion, fall in bed, and sleep for hours. Sarah had no one in her life; she was alone and felt abandoned by everyone.

About this time, a caravan of three families of cheapjacks arrived in Shillingstone to hawk their inventory of pots, pans, knives, dresses, gadgets and medicinal cures. As usual they created quite a stir, as several spouted out with an offensive sales pitch. After two days they left for Sturminster

Newton with the exception of one family whose wagon had a broken wheel. The village wheelwright agreed to repair their wheel in half a day. While waiting, they set up camp on the banks of the Stour River just north of town. When the family got their wagon back it was dark, and they decided to remain at their camp and leave in the morning.

That same night Sarah was exhausted and believed she was going crazy. She was having hallucinations and hearing voices with words she could not understand. Unable to sleep, she got up and looked out her old window. Through the bubbled glass Sarah was mesmerized gazing at a ghostly apparition of the moon. Spellbound by it she heard voices calling her. "Follow me, follow me." In the darkness of the night she left her cottage, and hastily walked down Blandford Road to the edge of the River Stour. When she looked up she saw a brightly cratered moon sliding in and out from behind ghostly clouds. As she wandered along the bank she continued to hear mysterious voices coming from strange people who stood around a bonfire casting eerie shadows and talking loudly. In fear, she ran down the bank and into the river trying to cross to the other side, but as she rushed into the water she lost her balance and fell forward, striking her head on a rock. A trickle of blood mixed with the flowing water.

The next morning a neighbor across the way thought it strange that the door to Sarah's cottage was wide open. She never left her door open, certainly not at night. Her neighbor entered with a lantern and had an ominous feeling something wasn't right. She decided to wait for Sarah to return, but when she was not back by noon the next day, she visited

Edith and told her what she had found. Edith was dumbfounded. When Sarah was despondent she always stayed in her cottage. Sergeant Wilson offered his help, but there was nothing to do but wait for her to return. By nightfall Sarah's cottage was again dark and empty. She was missing. They would have to wait until morning.

By noon the following day, many in Shillingstone were aware that Sarah was missing. The Major and Ellen saddled Boaz and Queen and rode the trails, pastures, roads and banks of the River Stour. All they found were the remnants of a camp fire. Other villagers searched in disorganized fashion. After three days it was determined that Sarah might never be found. All who knew her were confused and sad that she had disappeared.

CHEAPJACKS

With a chill in the air, the Warren family of cheapjacks had built a large bonfire and stood around with loud conversation, laughing and enjoying the warmth of the fire. One of the men saw a woman rush into the river and heard the splash of water, then silence. Curious, father and son went down to investigate and found a woman's body face down in the river. They turned her over and blood trickled from her forehead Mr. Warren and his son lifted her out and carried her to the warmth of the fire. Mrs. Warren rushed from their wagon with blankets to cover her wet body. She was unconscious but alive. They had no knowledge of who she was, only that she was helpless. They carried Sarah to their wagon where Mrs. Warren dressed her in dry clothes and put her in a bed.

At sunrise the group broke camp and traveled north on Blandford Road to Sturminster Newton. Covered with blankets, the strange woman remained unconscious. On the second day, she began to stir and gradually awoke. Mrs. Warren asked, "Ma'am, are you feeling better?"

The woman was confused and asked, "Where am I?"

Mrs. Warren explained, "Ma'am, we're a family of peddlers travelling north to sell our wares. You've been with us now for two days." After a pause she asked, "Ma'am, what's your name?"

Her mind was as blank as her stare. Trying to think, she replied, "I don't know."

"Do you remember falling in the river?"

"No."

"Do you remember where you live?

"No."

"What do you remember?"

"I don't know. Where am I?"

The woman had a blank stare on her face and was confused by the questions. She could only repeat, "I don't remember... I don't remember."

Mrs. Warren asked no more questions and encouraged her to eat something and get more rest. Perhaps later she would remember. Nothing helped. She didn't know her name, where she lived, her family, how old she was, or how she fell in the river. Her memory appeared to have been erased as clean as a schoolgirl's slate.

All along the way, starting with the village of Sturminster Newton, they asked people if they knew this woman they had saved from the Stour River. At every village they visited they got the same answer. No one knew her.

A month later, the Warren family still did not know what to do with the stranger. After some discussion, they agreed to take her with them, hoping somewhere along the way someone would recognize her. In the meantime she needed a name. After much discussion they settled on Eva. She appeared to be well-bred and well spoken. Eva would do just fine.

It was approaching a year since Sarah had disappeared. Life was back to normal for Edith, the sergeant and the Fletchers. On several occasions, Ellen invited the older couple to Hamilton House for dinner. After their meal, Ellen and Edith would huddle in the parlor and the two former soldiers would trade war stories in the library with cigars and brandy. During the evening Sarah's name came up, and they agreed they would never know what happened and likely never see her again.

THE PRINCE OF WALES

On several occasions, Edward, the Prince of Wales, took the royal train to Shillingstone's depot, and from there driven by coach to the estate of Lord Wolverton for a weekend of hunting.

On one of his hunting trips with Lord Wolverton, the prince became aware of a local honoree of the Victoria Cross, a Major Byron Fletcher. He was intrigued and requested that Major Fletcher and his wife be invited to Wolverton Hall on his next visit.

Six months later, a formal invitation for dinner with the Prince of Wales was extended to Major Byron and Lady Ellen Fletcher. Byron was surprised and Ellen was delighted. Their formal acceptance was handwritten and delivered to the residence of Lord Wolverton.

Over the years Ellen had attended many formal dinners with royalty, earls, barons and viscounts. Byron had attended military banquets and receptions, but never before had he received an invitation to a Royal dinner which included formal dress, etiquette, and protocol of which Byron was ignorant. Ellen began a fast course on the use of multiple knives, forks, spoons and wine glasses. There were also guidelines about conversation. Topics should be pleasant with no personal questions, or strong opinions on controversial subjects. If in doubt, she counseled, listen and watch others. He was especially nervous on learning he would not be seated next to his wife. Facing a fierce Maori warrior would be more comfortable than making a social faux pas during a formal dinner with the future king of England.

On the appointed evening a magnificent enclosed carriage with footmen arrived to carry Byron and Ellen to Wolverton Hall. Upon arrival, servants accepted their outer coats and guided them to a reception line in the great salon. The chief butler announced their entrance: "Ladies and gentlemen, Major Byron Fletcher and Lady Ellen Fletcher." They were greeted by Lord and Lady Wolverton, His Royal Highness the Prince of Wales and other important guests. Major Fletcher gave a nod and shook the prince's hand, while Lady Ellen curtsied. Byron noticed the men wore evening dress, black tails with tie. Their attire reminded him of a waddle of New Zealand penguins.

Major Fletcher's apparel was distinctive as he wore the formal uniform of the Dragoon Guard Light Horse Cavalry: scarlet waist dress jacket with gold mess knot epaulets embedded with the symbol of a crown, signifying the rank of major. Two gold bands on his sleeves showed his terms of service. Under his scarlet dress jacket he wore a white tuxedo shirt with a scarlet cummerbund and red bow tie. Dress trousers were navy blue with a wide red stripe down the side, complemented with polished short black boots. White cotton gloves completed the uniform. Around his neck the Victoria Cross was secured by a ribbon with the colors of the Union Jack. By any measure, he exemplified the best of England's officer corps.

Lady Ellen entered the room on his arm wearing a gorgeous cream-colored flowing gown reminiscent of a Greek goddess. Below her pearl choker, her dress slid slightly off her shoulders with long fluid tapered sleeves and cream gloves to her elbow. It was dramatic. Lady Ellen's long raven-colored hair was pulled on top of her head and was curled in an elegant style. She was young, stylish, and beautiful.

Dinner was a small affair with thirty guests. Rather than twelve courses, it was a modest eight with five different wines. Dessert was trifle and Battenberg cake, a favorite of His Royal Highness. During the dinner Major Fletcher had conversations with Lady Wolverton to his right and with her husband to his left. Directly across the table from him sat the Prince of Wales and his guest for the evening, Mrs. Lillie Langtry, a beautiful actress from the London stage. Lady Ellen was pleased with her husband's adroit handling of dinner etiquette.

Toward the conclusion of dessert, the Prince of Wales stood up and all conversation ceased. He announced, "I request that the ladies remain seated and the gentlemen, other than the major, rise. I propose a toast to Major Byron Fletcher, a recipient of the Queen's Victoria Cross for valor in the face of the enemy. He fought in India, China and New Zealand. He saved the life of a wounded major and defeated an enemy in battle. Ladies and gentlemen, I propose a toast to our guest of honor this evening, Major Byron Fletcher."

With a glass of wine in his hand he continued, "Ladies and gentlemen, a toast!" All raised their wine glasses and in unison repeated, "Major Fletcher, a toast!"

Byron was concerned about what would be next. His fears were confirmed when all the guests shouted, "Speech, speech!"

Major Fletcher stood erect with a military bearing and spoke, "Your Royal Highness... thank you for your kind words. I am proud to have served my country and your mother, Her Majesty the Queen. I am honored to wear the Victoria Cross as a symbol of this great nation. My father told me to keep speeches short and I have always listened to my father." After a titter of laughter he continued, "I thank each of you for your toast this evening…. Again, thank you." He took his seat to generous applause.

Ellen looked at him, smiled and whispered so he could read her lips, "I am so proud of you, and proud to be your wife."

The women withdrew to the drawing room and the men to the library for brandy and cigars. Conversation went late into the evening as Byron regaled the men with a few of his military adventures. After some nudging, Lady Wolverton declared that the ladies would like to retire for the night, a signal that the evening was over. Major Fletcher and Lady Ellen received their coats and rode back to Hamilton House. Sleep was not forthcoming as they talked about the evening well into the early morning. It had been a most wonderful experience

ALL IN THE FAMILY

For some time Eva was regarded as a rescued stranger with a new name, but she was not an intimate part of the cheapjack community. She had a different style of speaking, an expansive vocabulary and a polished manner, but no memory of her former life. The Warren family simply accepted her as she now lived a cheapjack way of life.

Eva's memory was like a picture frame minus a picture. She had no knowledge of the cheapjack's reputation for selling cheap and shoddy goods. They peddled new and used pots, pans, and knives, as well as clothing for men, women, and children. They also sold medicinal products including a remedy called Dr. Allcock's porous plaster to cure chest colds. For aches and pains they sold Sir. John Hill's Pectoral Balsam of Honey which contained tree resin, honey and nitrous opium. Most medicinal cures came in small bottles which allowed a substantial inventory to be carried in a small space in their wagon.

Some cheapjacks excelled at bamboozling. The greatest purveyors of this skullduggery were palmists and fortune tellers. Most of the time they plied their trade during festivals and fairs near larger towns. They would set up a tent and invite patrons to enter for a reading while a barker shouted out, "Clergy promise a solution for your afterlife, we promise advice and solutions for your present life!" For attention, some would dress up in top hat and tails or others as an Indian maharaja. After a group gathered around the tent, they were enticed to enter one at a time. Advice came only after a coin was placed in the palmist's or fortune teller's hand. After a reading, a client was encouraged to tell others of his or her astonishing experience. Talented palmists and fortune tellers made a good living.

Others were travelling gamblers, promising an easy way to make a fortune. Some played games like cup and ball or shell games asking patrons to guess which one of three shells had a small ball under it. At first players were allowed to win. As the stakes got higher winners quickly became losers. These bamboozlers gathered a crowd quickly, took their money quickly, and departed quickly.

Cheapjacks were much like honeybees. If honey was desired, it was necessary to put up with annoying buzzing bees and periodic stings. These travelers were often annoying, but they provided products needed for small rural farmers. On occasion, buyers were stung. Still they were accepted by folks in small isolated farms and hamlets as it was difficult to travel to distant market towns.

The quality of their products was as cheap as the price. Cash or barter made little difference. In cramped wagons packed with products, the Warrens traveled the length and breadth of England and Wales on coarse uneven roads and primitive trails. They stay overnight on any rural space they could find. Camping with small farmers was mutually beneficial. Cheapjacks often bartered products for extended days of camping in a secure environment. It was a difficult life, but the only one the Warren family knew.

Eva was now a cheapjack and living a peripatetic life. She had no doubt about her welcome by the Warrens and their son, Ben, but everywhere they traveled it was obvious she had not been born a cheapjack. When asked, Mr. Warren told the story of her rescue and memory loss. It was a tale told many times over. She was welcomed, but was an outsider.

Ben had his own problems. At 28 he was not married. Every attempt he had made was unsuccessful. Living a nomadic life made it difficult to meet young women and at his age he was competing with men who were younger. He had not found a wife, but that would soon change.

After traveling with the Warrens for eight months, Eva was pregnant.

Ben confessed that he was the father and rather than be angry, his parents were delighted. After a family conference it was agreed that Ben and Eva should get married.

However, a formal marriage blessed by the church was not possible. Eva had no knowledge of where or when she had been born. In the society of cheapjacks there was little stigma in living as husband and wife without a legal marriage. Ben and Eva's relationship was accepted. They possessed a love and commitment for each other that joined them as a couple.

Six months later Eva gave birth to a beautiful baby girl. They named her Lilly, after Ben's grandmother. With four adults and a new baby, the Warren wagon was crowded. With some help from his parents Ben planned to buy his own wagon. After searching for several months they were fortunate to find an old wagon that needed only minor repairs. The main box extended over four large wheels and the sides connected to a curved roof, creating more space. A rear door set off to one side provided interior space for a cast iron stove and a small kitchen area. One interior wall had a double bunk, and the other a hinged bed that folded down for Ben and Eva. Closets, drawers, cabinets, and shelves were everywhere, inside and out. Adequate light came from windows on the front and back. To pull their heavy wagon they were able to purchase a couple of old farm horses. One horse pulled the wagon half the time while the other was tied to the back of the wagon. Rather than ride, Ben usually walked beside the horse and only rode on the wagon only during inclement weather. Ben, Eva, and Lilly were now on their own.

Their journey began outside the village of Blackpool on the west coast of England north of Liverpool. They planned to move south visiting small hamlets and farms. Normally they were able to travel 5 to 10 miles a day. They had gathered a good inventory of products that would be of interest to small farmers and poor farm laborers. As they approached a small hamlet Ben would hang pots and pans on hooks outside their wagon and attach bells to the harness of his horse. It was a vivid way to announce that a travelling family was arriving to sell their wares. The unique wagon was itself a point of interest. Ben searched for a grassy area to park, set out a table and displayed some of his merchandise. Eva handled the money and Ben did the bartering. It was like they had brought a small village fair as people gathered around, curious about what they were selling. It was not unusual for farm workers to ask if Ben had anything for aches and pains. He had recently purchased bottles of universal snake oil, known as "A Miracle Elixir" which included cocaine, morphine or opium. It was a good seller.

Eva was coming into her own as she had observed Ben's mother and father working together to survive on their many travels. While she mothered little Lilly, she managed all the domestic chores necessary for a family of three as the wagon bounced and swayed as they moved from village to village. She helped Ben in purchasing inventory, noting what sold and at what price. Even when Ben did the bartering, he relied on Eva for advice.

After six months on the road they faced their first serious conflict with villagers. They were travelling along the Welsh border, and decided to take a small road leading west toward Wales. For a month they visited small farms and hamlets without a problem, even though it was a challenge to understand the Welsh accents. When they entered a very small village called Llanwrtyd Wells that changed. It seemed like the entire population came out and shouted, "Get out, you robbers, cheats and thieves!" A group of fifteen men surrounded their wagon and told them that they were not welcome. Ben was stuck as he couldn't turn around on the narrow street. When he stopped, Eva came down the back stairs holding Lilly's small hand. When the crowd saw that they were a family they became quiet as Eva explained that they were not gamblers; they only came to sell some of their wares. A leader of the group came forward to explain their anger. He told Eva and Ben that the previous week a man with a small wagon arrived and set up a table to gamble and to play a game with three shells. At first a few villagers won, but as the stakes got higher every player lost his hard-earned money. It was a scam where no one could win. When the gambler was discovered cheating, he quickly jumped into his wagon and hustled out of town. The town's people were wary of being taken again, but their anger subsided when they found that Ben and Eva had only come to sell items they might need. The spokesman corrected their mistake and welcomed them to their village. Those who appeared to be enemies became friends.

After their experience in Wales, Ben and Eva returned to England and proceeded south toward Cornwall. By this time they had been on the road for two years. On their travels they had met other cheapjack families, giving them an opportunity to socialize and exchange gossip. On one such occasion Eva disclosed to Ben and others that she was expecting a second child. All were delighted.

For the next eight months they travelled hundreds of miles over rough gravel roads and narrow lanes. They were tolerated, ignored or welcomed by the villagers they met along these many miles. Some days they had good sales and others days only a few items sold. They were approaching Willard in Dorset in beautiful pastoral country when Eva believed her baby was about to arrive. When they reached Willard, Ben sought a midwife to assist with the birth. With her assistance a second girl was born. They named her Ruth.

Two days later they were on the road again and found themselves in the heart of Cornwall's mining district. Ben had been told that miners were paid low wages and risked injuries, aches and pains. He had a tonic that would relieve both soreness and pain. It was a new "Miracle Elixir" of snake oil with opium included. It sold very well.

Most of Cornwall's west coast was rugged terrain with the Atlantic Ocean breaking against jagged walls of rock. Mining towers and smoke stacks dotted the shore line. It was beautiful and dangerous. A short way inland a different scene revealed beautiful undulating pastoral landscapes crisscrossed with narrow hedgerow lanes which made it difficult to pass oncoming wagons. After several weeks in Cornwall's 'Land's End' they turned around and started north to other parts of England. They crossed hundreds of miles on rural roads over the next four years when one day Eva told Ben that she was expecting their third child. Ben was hoping for a son. At full term Eva gave birth to a healthy boy. Ben had always liked the name Thomas and Eva agreed. By now Lilly was seven years old and Ruth was almost four. Their wagon was crowded with a new baby and two small children. Motherhood took up most of Eva's time and energy.

When Thomas was born they were near the market town of Bedale, North Yorkshire in northern England. Here they decided to turn around and return south. The midlands of England was farming country with a population that accepted cheapjacks and the prices of their inventory.

By now Ben and Eva were doing well financially. However in recent years they became aware that they had to cross over an increasing number of railroad crossings. Twice they had to stop and wait for an oncoming train to pass in front of them. Rail service across England created the availability of better products and prices than those offered by Ben and Eva. In the future it was likely that fewer caravans would be crossing the country, which meant that there would be fewer peddlers on the roads. Ben was determined to be one of the few who still travelled the roads of the English countryside.

RETURN TO SHILLINGSTONE

For over ten years Ben and his family had traveled hundreds of miles through England's heartland. From all those distances his wagon had taken a beating and two wheels were in need of major repair. On their journey south they were about to enter Sturminster Newton. Ben remembered a wheelwright in Shillingstone who had done good work for his father years before. They were only five miles from Shillingstone, so he decided to have the same man check the hubs on his wagon and replace several broken spokes.

After examining the condition of Ben's old wagon, the wheelwright agreed to make the repairs. Since he was busy, it would take one or two days. He recommended the Warrens stay at the Old Ox Inn, which Ben arranged. Walking to the inn with her children, Eva did not recognize anyone or anything in Shillingstone.

Soon the children became unhappy at the inn as they were stuck in a small room. Since it was a nice morning, Eva took them for a walk down Blandford Road. They strolled past the grocer's shop, remembering to pick up some items on the way back. They passed the post office which was next to the blacksmith's forge and the wheelwright's shop. The children were fascinated by the bellows which created a searing fire and dense black smoke as the blacksmith pumped it by hand. He enjoyed the attention of the children watching as their eyes widened at the sizzle of red hot metal when he plunged the metal into a slack tub of water. While their mother stood watching, Andy looked at her and was puzzled. This woman reminded him of Sarah, only older and fuller around the middle. Was that possible or was it just his imagination?

Working on Ben's wagon was putting the wheelwright behind in his work, so he asked Ben to carry the damaged rim over to Andy's blacksmith shop. While Andy worked on the rim, he asked Ben, "You been in these parts before?"

"Not for...a long time. Years back your wheelwright made some repairs on my father's wagon as we passed through."

"Remember how long ago?"

"No... maybe, ten years, maybe more... thinking about it, my wife may have come from here abouts."

"Were those her children watching me at the forge?"

"Yup, that's her, Eva, two girls and a boy. Hard for 'em, cooped up."

"Nice family, Ben. I should have this rim back on your wheel in a bit."

"Much appreciated."

At home later that night, Andy could not help but think more about seeing Ben's wife. Could that possibly be Sarah? Even older, she looked much like Sarah. Ben had said that she came from around this area about a decade ago. Andy remembered how he felt about her and wanted to know if his suspicions might be true. He decided to visit Sarah's Aunt Edith and in the morning tell her about meeting Eva.

At midmorning, Andy took a break from his forge and went to Edith's cottage. What he told Edith was received with disbelief. How could it be, after all these years? Andy wondered if Edith would stop by the Old Ox Inn to see for herself. Edith said she would think about it. Andy returned to work, frustrated that Edith didn't show much interest in what he had told her.

After Andy left, Edith thought to herself, what did she have to lose? She shared Andy's story with Sergeant Wilson, and they agreed to make some excuse to visit the Old Ox Inn. When they entered they were surprised at what they saw. Eva was holding her youngest child while the other two were running around the inn like out of control little monkeys. In the confusion Edith introduced herself and the sergeant. Eva introduced herself, but did not recognize Edith. While trying not to stare, Edith thought Eva did look somewhat like Sarah. She then suggested that Eva and her children walk to their cottage to play and work off some excess energy. It was a thoughtful invitation and readily accepted.

Arriving home, Edith made tea and sandwiches. The children settled down while eating. Edith whispered to the sergeant to take the children for a walk to Hamilton House and tell the major what had just happened. The older children were excited to have a soldier march them off to meet another soldier.

When they arrived at Hamilton House, both major and Ellen were home. When the sergeant told Edith's story, the major was skeptical. Ellen took the children to the stable to feed a carrot to their pony, so the men could talk. Sergeant Wilson suggested Byron and Ellen stop by his cottage when he returned with the children and they agreed. When they arrived, Eva introduced herself, but did not recognize Byron. The children were soon bored, and they returned to the inn.

After Eva and the children left, the two couples sat in stunned silence. Was this woman Sarah? After all these years how could this possibly be? According to her husband, she had no memory of her past life. Byron recognized the dimples Sarah had from childhood, and he believed Eva was actually Sarah. She was alive after all these years! Eventually, they all agreed that Sarah had returned. Now what should they do? They decided to visit Ben and Eva the next morning.

The following morning when they arrived at the inn the family was gone. Byron asked the innkeeper about them and was told that the father had settled his bill the night before and they had left before sunrise. He had no idea where they were headed. Byron was sorely disappointed and didn't know what to do. Sarah had come home, and now she and her children were gone. Would he ever find her again?

With their wagon repaired, Ben, Eva and the children left Shillingstone prior to dawn and continued north on the road to Sturminster Newton to market their goods. The repairs and the expense of the Old Ox Inn came close to depleting their meager savings. Ahead were long days, rough roads and living on the edge of survival. Eva cared for their three small children as best she could in their cramped wagon packed with goods. In most towns they stayed one day, others two or three days for village festivals or celebrations. Folks accepted that peddlers were just trying to make a living.

HOUSE OF COMMONS

In their second year back home, Ellen gave birth to a healthy baby boy, with a wisp of rust-colored hair. He was named David Howard Fletcher, after Ellen's great-grandfather and Byron's father. The tranquility they had enjoyed was considerably altered with the birth of little David. Ellen made the decision to care for her baby rather than hire a nursemaid, and as a result the infant controlled Hamilton House, much to the delight of his parents.

Unexpectedly, Byron became a political figure in the village. When asked to serve on the Parish Council, he demurred, but to no avail. His name was placed on the ballot and he was elected. In a short time, the major learned that a village parish did not function like the military, but he was able to adjust. With his world travel and military experience he became a valuable resource. When elected chairman, he jumped in enthusiastically, or as much as Ellen and David would allow. Being part of a Parish Council had not been on Major Fletcher's agenda, but it was something he began to relish. Everywhere he went, he was stopped for advice, or words of encouragement or simple casual conversation. Shillingstone was now a small village that had a man of stature, whose influence would go well beyond their borders.

Having survived the torrid heat of India, having fought religious zealots in China and come face to face with tattooed Maori warriors in New Zealand, Byron now basked in the peace and warmth of family life. There was nothing more he would wish for, but his tranquility would not be long lasting.

A representative of the Conservative party visited the major and asked him to run for Parliament from the West Dorset constituency. The Conservatives had done poorly in recent elections against the Liberal Party. The major was in the main a conservative, but remained open minded on a variety of matters. After a lengthy discussion with the Conservative Party representative, he expressed some interest. He wanted to consult Ellen before he made a final decision and when he did, she encouraged him to run and win.

Ellen lived with her father for most of her youth, and she was familiar with the world of politics. Her father was a peer and was thereby a member of the House of Lords. As a result, members of both houses of Parliament had tramped through their home on a regular basis to consult with her father. Ellen had a good understanding of the time, energy and public attention involved in a political career. The possibility of Byron becoming a Member of Parliament was both daunting and exciting. Politically, this would be a giant step forward for the major. After extensive consultation with appropriate members of the Conservative Party, Byron decided to make a run for the West Dorset seat.

Sixty days was not a long time to campaign for a seat as a Member of Parliament in Her Majesty's Government. Organization and command were the major's strengths, so Byron was eager to jump into the political fray and did so with alacrity. He organized a committee of men and women from every borough of West Dorset, every trade union and every social organization. Other workers made signs and had leaflets printed. Byron saddled up Boaz to personally meet as many people as possible. In larger communities he harnessed Boaz to a carriage and traveled with Ellen and, on occasion, little David. No candidate for this office had ever met so many voters face to face. In his campaign message, Byron pointed out that he was born the son of a farmer and he was still that same farmer's son. Most voters were or had been sons of farmers. After skillfully building momentum, the major handily defeated the liberal candidate and was sworn in as a Member of Parliament.

In June of 1873 the major attended his first opening session for the Houses of Parliament of the United Kingdom. It was a pageant to behold. A parade of peers wearing their scarlet robes trimmed with white ermine entered the lower chamber and filled every seat, leaving no room for elected Members of Parliament. In contrast to the colorful garb of peers, elected members wore ordinary black robes, and were given the privilege of standing behind the seated peers. Both chambers of Parliament awaited the arrival of Queen Victoria to open the session. Upon her arrival she was escorted to the chamber by the Lord Great Chamberlain. Queen Victoria wore the Imperial State Crown and the Parliamentary Robe of State which included an impressive 18-foot crimson velvet cape lined with ermine and trimmed with gold lace. As ruling monarch, she sat on her throne before the assembly. Following tradition, she gave the Queen's Speech, declared Parliament open, and promptly returned to Buckingham Palace.

Byron and Ellen were more fortunate than many rural Members of Parliament as her father years ago had purchased a town house in central London. They now made this their home when Parliament was in session. Byron had an office in the town house where he could work at the end of each day. Now his priority was to work at improving the lives of the voters who had elected him to this position. He was as diligent an MP as he had been as an adjutant officer.

After two years as a back bencher, he was asked to speak to the House of Commons on behalf of his Conservative party. This was a rare opportunity extended to few back benchers. He spoke eloquently on the need for a new policy in managing the empire's colonies.

His recommendations were well-received by a senior MP and former Colonial Secretary, Henry Herbert, the fourth Earl of Carnarvon of Highclere Castle, who had been a peer for many years. Herbert was often in the middle of political debates and was a sponsor of numerous important laws. When he was colonial secretary he had successfully guided the British Canadian Colony to independence with passage of the British North American Act of 1867. As the fourth Earl he was a liberal-leaning member of the Conservative Party and a leading advocate for colonial federation with England's colonies. While no longer the colonial secretary, he continued to advise his successors on such issues. One concern was New Zealand. He felt information he received on the relationship of New Zealand's Maori with the colonial government was not reliable. He had recently learned that Major Fletcher had served in New Zealand and was familiar with the Maori culture. He seemed a capable young man for what the Earl had in mind.

HIGHCLERE CASTLE

At the end of the 1882 session of the House of Commons, the fourth Earl of Carnarvon invited Byron and Ellen to dine at Highclere Castle. It would be a convenient stop halfway between London and Shillingstone. So his invitation was graciously accepted. Waiting at the station for them was an exquisite carriage with footmen who whisked them off to the castle. On the way, Byron was thinking he was about to visit a different world than his humble home in Shillingstone. Entering the estate they saw a magnificent castle surrounded by acres of flawless lawns, countless shrubs and trees.

They were greeted warmly by the fourth Earl and his wife, Countess Elizabeth Catherine Herbert. Beyond the large entry doors they entered a long hallway with high columns supporting a vaulted ceiling. Just ahead was the Earl's favorite room, the grand salon. A focal point was an immense stone fireplace which had been hand-carved by skilled artisans. A portrait of the Earl in his Peer's robe hung on the left of the fireplace, and a portrait of Lady Elizabeth Carnarvon on the right. Although the salon was large, the furnishings and warmth of the hearth provided a cozy atmosphere. Conversation flowed freely as they enjoyed a glass of wine.

When dinner was announced, they entered a large formal dining room replete with portraits of past and present family members hung around all the walls. On an end wall was a large portrait that extended from floor to ceiling portraying a nobleman splendidly mounted on a majestic white stallion. It dominated the room and Byron wondered who he was. After a sumptuous dinner and a variety of wines, Lady Elizabeth Carnarvon and Lady Ellen retired to the drawing room for tea and conversation. Byron and the Earl adjourned to the library, which was used as the Earl's withdrawing room. Before cigars and brandy, Byron wished to know the identity of the man in the large portrait, but he didn't want to show his ignorance. He commented, "Sir, I was impressed with the large portrait in the dining room,"

Before he could say anything more the Earl injected, "You mean the portrait of King Charles the First?"

Relieved, Byron responded, "Yes…yes King Charles."

The Earl continued, "That was originally painted in 1636 and has been in Highclere Castle for as long as I can remember." he added, "Unfortunately, Charles did not fare very well. Now let's have some brandy." Over brandy and cigars the Earl shared his concerns about New Zealand. Maori leaders were dissatisfied with their treatment by the colonial government. He wanted someone like Major Fletcher to visit New Zealand, define the problems and make recommendations to resolve them. Byron was surprised and honored to be asked and indicated he could only say that he would give his answer within a week. Time had passed quickly and everyone was ready to turn in for the night.

Servants had unpacked their travel bags in a bedroom selected by the housekeeper. It was a large room on the second level with two floor-to-ceiling windows. A writing desk was in front of the left window and the right window had a table with a washbasin, a water pitcher, and face and hand towels. Their bed had been turned down and a warm fire glowed in the fireplace. A series of candles around the room provided ample light. The bedroom was well-appointed with family portraits, drapes and furniture. Byron and Ellen felt like royalty. They slept well.

The next morning they joined their hosts for a breakfast of boiled eggs, bacon, bread, fish, fruits, jam, toast and tea. They had a delightful visit and thanked the Earl and his wife for their superb hospitality. Estate staff provided a carriage to take them to the rail station for their trip back to Shillingstone.

On the train, Byron told Ellen about the Earl's request that he investigate problems with the Maori in New Zealand. He told her "The trip would take at least six months away from home. My duties as MP for West Dorset would be neglected, but more important, I would be away from you and our son for too long. I cannot bring myself to accept his request."

Ellen was silent for some time. Then she said, "Byron, you must go. You will be miserable if you don't. Living with a husband who is unhappy is worse that missing him for six or more months. It is a cause close to your heart and you must do it. Lord Carnarvon will see to your parliamentary duties. It is a mission of mercy for the Maori."

Before Byron could make a decision, he wanted to think about all the implications. Was he willing to make this sacrifice to improve the lives of the Maori? Would it really make a difference? If he did not go would he have lingering regrets? Usually Byron decided quickly and confidently, but not now. It would have been easier if Ellen had just said no.

Over the next several days Ellen knew that he was having difficulty deciding what to do. Finally one day she made tea and they sat down in the drawing room and she began, "Byron, one of the reasons I married you was that you care more for others than you do for yourself. Now you need to do this as much for yourself as for anyone else. I love you dearly and have your interest at heart. Go, fulfill your duty. I will pray for your safety."

He replied, "My dear Ellen, thank you, thank you for your support and love. I will miss you and little David."

A LONG ROAD

Over the next fifteen years, the Warren family travelled all over England and Wales. Life was difficult. As their children grew they were unhappy in a cramped wagon. Any place would be better than how they lived. When they grew older they spent less time in the wagon during the day. Often they either walked behind the wagon or alongside their father. At times Eva also followed behind the wagon with all the children. When they stopped for the day, the two oldest, Lilly and Thomas were responsible for feeding and watering the horses and fastening them to the trailer for the night.

Lilly was the first to leave. By nature she was impatient and impulsive. As the oldest she resented sharing space with Ruth and Thomas. At fifteen Lilly decided to leave her family at her first opportunity. It came at a fair in the village of Rye, Sussex. She fancied a young man she met at a Coconut Shire booth and he responded favorably to her advances. He was five years older and told Lilly that he was an apprentice smithy in his father's forge. They spent as much time together as possible in the midst of a bustling crowd of fairgoers. On the last day Lilly told him she was in love and wanted to run away and get married. He was in love with her and agreed. When it was time for Ben and Eva to leave they were unable to find Lilly. They waited an extra day, but were unsuccessful. Their only hope was to leave a message with the Parish Council and ask for their help. Ben and Eva knew in their hearts they would never see Lilly again. With a heavy heart and with Ruth and Thomas on board they turned west toward England's coast.

Traveling down a rough road all four were jostled around in the wagon with differing moods. Lilly was gone. No one knew how unhappy she was or how determined she was to escape. Ben and Eva were silent in their sadness. Ruth and Thomas were also silent, but were glad she was gone, making more room for them. Ben and Eva now turned their thoughts to Ruth and Thomas. What will happen to them? Will they try to run away as well?

After traveling west for six months, they found themselves outside the village of Blackpool on the shore of the Irish Sea. Here they decided to rest, recuperate and replenish their inventory. Ben and Thomas decided to take a long walk through the village to the coast. Along the way Thomas became fascinated by the different patterns of thatched roofs that enhanced their cottages. For the past two years he wanted to get away from his life of travel, find a job and stay in one place. He had just discovered what he wanted to do. He was fortunate to meet a thatcher who was roofing a village home. Blackpool was growing and the thatcher had more work than he could accept. Ben asked the hard-working man if he needed any help. Indeed he did. Ben introduced himself and his son Thomas, who was interested in how homes had thatched roofs. After an extended conversation the thatcher, he agreed to teach fourteen-year-old Thomas the thatching trade. Ben and Eva were disappointed that Thomas wanted to leave, but they were sure this was what he wanted to do. They were confident that he would be well-cared for, however they were not certain that they would ever see him again.

Rested, the remaining three were back on the roads and trails of rural England. Ben thought they should travel the Midlands again. Ruth, now sixteen, was also not happy to be jostled around in their wagon anymore, but was pleased to have more room for herself. Over the next year they had gone east and began to circle around to go back west. About this time they were outside the village of Shrewsbury, which appeared to be a bustling market town. It would be an opportunity to restock their inventory with goods to sell in the coming year. It was here that Ruth decided to leave her parents. Lilly and Thomas had been successful in departing and she wanted to do so as well. While Ben was negotiating with village suppliers, Eva took Ruth for a walk around the area to view the variety of village homes. As they strolled down one of the lanes an older lady was out watering her flowers. She had a charming array of plants and shrubs that complemented her delightful cottage. Eva loved her flowers and appreciated the colors and variety of her plants. The lady noticed her interest and she gave Eva an appreciative smile. That was sufficient them to start a friendly chat. The woman noticed that they were visitors and invited the pair in for tea, which they graciously accepted.

Their hostess introduced herself as Sophia Glanville, a widow for the second time. She told Eva that her last husband, Edward, was a railroad man who was killed in an accident several years after they were married. At that time she had three young girls, but now they are married and on their own. Eva expressed her sympathy on the death of her husband. During tea Sophia's nephew Stephen stopped for a visit and Sophia introduced him to her guests. He was a handsome young man, a little older than Ruth. Almost immediately there was a connection between them. When it was time for Ruth to leave, Stephen was clearly disappointed. Sophia had noticed, and invited Ruth and her parents for dinner the next day.

Ruth could hardly wait for tomorrow. Neither could Stephen. The Warrens arrived for dinner at Sophia's cottage where Ben was introduced to their hostess. By design, Sophia sat her nephew next to Ruth. She was aware that Stephen had never found a young lady to his liking, until now. Eva, Sophia and even Ben picked up on the eagerness between Stephen and Ruth. It was as though they were the only two people at the table. The evening grew late and it was time to leave. Stephen asked Ben if he could come by the next morning and visit Ruth. Ben said he would ask Eva, already knowing the answer. Eva agreed and a time was set for Stephen to visit. Ruth was smitten with Stephen and Steven was besotted with Ruth.

The next morning Stephen stopped to talk to his aunt about his dilemma. He was in love with Ruth, and she would be leaving with her parents in a few days. He asked, "What can I do?"

Sophia had anticipated this situation and responded, "What would you think if I asked her parents to allow her to live with me until you both decide what you want to do?" He could hardly believe what his aunt said and was thrilled by her suggestion.

The next morning Stephen met Ruth at their caravan. While visiting he asked Ben if he could take Ruth for a walk around the village. During their walk Stephen told Ruth about the conversation he had with his aunt and the offer, if Ruth's parents agreed. Ruth was ecstatic about the prospect of living with Sophia.

Back at their wagon, Ruth told her parents about Sophia's invitation. They wanted the best for her and agreed that they should meet and clarify the arrangement.

At Sophia's cottage there was ample nervousness and anticipation. Ben wanted to know more about Stephen. Sophia looked at her nephew and suggested that he speak for himself. Nervously he proceeded, "My father has been a boot maker for many years. He's training me to follow him, which I am doing. I told him about Ruth and he was pleased." Sophia confirmed that Stephen came from a good family and believed that Ruth might be just the right person for him. It was agreed that Ruth would live with Sophia and be under her care for up to six months. During that time Ruth and Stephen could decide on their future. They were elated. Ben, Eva and Sophia agreed to communicate by telegraph on any future decisions.

After many years of traveling with their children Ben and Eva would now be roaming over rural country roads by themselves. They were saddened but satisfied that their three children would be able to find their way in life.

Eva had turned sixty and looked her age. Her beautiful hair had thinned and turned gray and white. Years of sun, cold weather, rain and wind had placed lines across her face that obscured her once beautiful dimples. She moved slowly and with a slight stoop. However, a frail body belied her inner strength that had carried through the past thirty years. It would be needed in the years ahead.

Ben had always been a strong, hard-working, man, but thousands of miles had taken their toll on his body. Ten years previously he had injured his back getting the wagon out of a ditch. His life as a cheapjack was becoming more challenging and difficult with every passing year. A worn-out wagon constantly needed repairs and they had gone through more than dozens of old horses over countless thousands of miles. Ben was ready to get off the road and find a home that was more than a wagon.

A NEW HOME

Of the hundreds of villages that they had passed through, Ben and Eva remembered a small village called Thistleton in Rutland. It was a friendly town with a population of less than one hundred souls. Ben remembered that there were several abandoned cottages that could be repaired and made livable. Most were small stone houses with thatched roofs. Some had doors and windows missing, but appeared to be solid.

They found their way back to Thistleton and were pleased they had been remembered by some of the villagers. The small town had a public house, a vacant carpet factory, and 28 homes, of which three were empty. Of the three, one had possibilities. What would he need to make it livable? When Ben contacted the owner he was told that if he made repairs, his rent would be cheap. That was good news.

They chose a small cottage with a bedroom, a roomy kitchen and a fireplace. Like most of the homes, it was built of stone with a thatched roof in need of repair. A front door hung askew on one hinge and two windows were missing. Eva was excited that they would finally be settled in one place without the earth constantly moving under her feet. In a short time the needed repairs were made and they moved into the cottage with their meager furniture. Eva had found two old windows which Ben installed, along with hinges for the door. Villagers were so pleased to have them move in that they made it a community project of fixing their roof. Eva could not have been more content. For the first time she could make curtains for the windows, plant flowers in the front yard and enjoy the warmth and light of a fireplace.

After miles and miles of travel over many years they had finally found their little piece of heaven. They had travelled through the searing heat and humidity of the summer, the cold and driving snow in winter and on roads that were almost impassable. It had been a harsh and difficult life. They had lost Lilly forever. While Thomas lived in Blackpool it was unlikely they would ever see him again. The only child they could contact was Ruth. For the first time they could remember, they were finally in their own home and it didn't move.

One afternoon in April of 1897, the sky turned dark, and a wind from the east caused tree branches to bend causing leaves to fly through the air like green butterflies. In the distance thunder rumbled and rolled across the sky as rain pelted down on their cottage. When the darkness of night descended, Ben and Eva went to bed. Ben slept soundly while Eva was uneasy and was unable to sleep.

In the middle of the night, bolts of lightning shot across the sky, followed by horrendous claps of thunder like a cacophony of cannons that were constantly booming. Driven by the wind, rain savagely assaulted their cottage and the thunder seemed to make the very ground shake. Eva looked at Ben, who was sound asleep. She was restless and finally got up to look out a window to watch the lightening flash. Rain was cascading down the outside of their old window like a fast flowing stream. Small bubbles of air in the window's glass seemed to move around in circles and the uneven glass appeared to ripple like waves on a pond of water. A bolt of lightning exploded like an arrow piercing the ground just beyond the front of their home. In a split second thunder boomed, creating a concussion which shook the building and rattled the windows. In absolute terror Eva fell back on her bed in shock. She had difficulty breathing, and when she opened her eyes, dark spots danced around in front of them. Ben had heard the last frightful explosion and awakened. Eva sat on her bed traumatized, in a trance, unable to speak. Ben asked, "Eva, are you all right?" She could not answer. Perhaps she didn't hear him. He spoke louder, "Eva…Eva, do you hear me? Are you all right?"

"I hear you."

"Is something wrong?"

"…No."

"Can you say something?"

"…Yes."

"Say something, please… please, say something!"

"I remember."

"You remember?"

"…I remember."

"What do you remember?"

"I remember my name."

"Your name is Eva."

"No…my name is Sarah."

NEW ZEALAND II

Fortunately, sailing from England to New Zealand now took less than 50 days. A new steel hulled commercial steamship, the SS Doric, would sail the distance with comfortable accommodations for the major and Boaz. Without challenging seas they arrived in Wellington, New Zealand, in 46 days. Waiting at the harbor was Ellen's father, having been alerted by his daughter to Byron's arrival. He was delighted to see Byron and to hear details about his new grandson. The commander had seven months left on his assignment, and he offered all the assistance his son-in-law would request. He was aware that Byron was in New Zealand on a government assignment and would be communicating with Governor Lieutenant-General Sir William Jervis. After paying his respects to the governor, and with an understanding of his assignment, Byron rode Boaz to the regimental headquarters and settled in to the officers' quarters to rest for several days.

Most of the Maori population still resided north of Auckland, so Byron and Boaz took a costal steamer north. After a day plying the waters on the west coast of New Zealand they arrived at Auckland Harbor. It was much improved from his first visit seventeen years ago. Byron saddled Boaz, who wore his years very well, and headed for the Blandford army base. He could not believe the first person he met. Byron was astonished to receive a salute from Sergeant Matiu. As promised, the New Zealand government had paid his expenses to enter and train in Camp Aldershot, England. Sergeant Matiu was surprised and delighted as he not been told that Major Fletcher had returned. Byron could think of no better companion for his journey than Sergeant Matiu.

Although the North Island was still primitive, there was now a road from Auckland to the north end of the island. His plan was to ride from Auckland to the Bay of Islands and further, if time allowed. Sergeant Matiu would be of great help on this journey. Byron travelled in civilian clothes and Matiu in his uniform as a sergeant in the New Zealand army. They would represent the government and the military.

Everywhere they went they drew attention and were invited to stop and visit. Tribal leaders and individual Maori felt free to express their concerns and complaints. For the Maori the issue was all about land and respect. Europeans had taken most of their land and they felt cheated. In varying degrees the message Major Byron heard was the same. As they rode a trail through the mountainous terrain and heavily treed forests, they realized this discontent was felt by a majority of the natives.

One place Byron was anxious to visit was the Te Waimate Mission House with Reverend Richard Davis and his wife as he had pleasant memories of the time he had spent with them. Byron and Matiu were invited to spend as much time there as they wished. He informed the Reverend of his purpose and would be pleased to hear his view on the Maori discontent. Reverend Davis told the same story. The Maori continue to be angry over what happened to their land, leaving them feeling like strangers with little hope that anything would change. Doing battle with the Europeans had changed nothing other than diminishing their population. Fighting was no longer a realistic option. After hours of conversation everyone agreed that it was time to relax and enjoy the mission and to hear about some progress in converting the Maori and the benefit that accrued for everyone. Reverend Davis told many stories of his experiences which Byron was pleased to hear.

After the visit to the mission Byron decided that he had heard enough so he and Sergeant Matiu boarded a coastal steamer at the Bay of Islands to sail back to Auckland. Once there he expressed his appreciation to Matiu for his help and how wonderful it was to see him again. He then took the first steamer back to Wellington.

In Wellington Byron had a conference with the governor and shared some of his observations and the concerns of the Maori which the governor greatly appreciated. The time it would take to sail back to England would allow Byron to form recommendations for the 4th Earl of Carnarvon and the House of Commons.

Byron arrived back in Portsmouth almost five months to the day he had left. He and Boaz were anxious to be home in Shillingstone. He had sent a telegram to Ellen, so she and David met him at the station with some exciting news. In three months David would have either a brother or sister. Safely back home Byron was delighted that they would be having a second child. Ellen had a glow unique to a mother with child. For Byron, it was time to finish his New Zealand assignment and report to Lord Carnarvon at his London office.

After a week's rest Byron took the train to London and the House of Commons. Lord Carnarvon was expecting him and was anxious to hear his report. First, Byron extended a greeting from the governor of New Zealand, with appreciation for his addressing issues with the Maori population. Then Byron said, "Sir, while there are many issues, I believe there have been essentially two. Ownership of land continues to be the major problem with the Maori as it was their land and it was taken from them. A second issue has been respect. Truthfully, respect would be difficult to come by when the Maori, up to recent years, practiced cannibalism, infanticide and beheading. As odious as it may sound, such practices have been endemic in their culture for centuries."

"Major, your points are well taken. Now how do you believe our government should respond?"

"Sir, addressing the first issue would help with the second issue. Admit that many Maori have been cheated out of their land. Develop a program of restitution for property taken surreptitiously, and set aside large protected areas for the Maori population."

Byron had thought long and hard about the question of respect. Would it be possible for the Maori to change their culture? He commented further, "Sir, on the second question I believe the concept of a carrot and stick approach would be appropriate. Demonstrate the benefits of education, training, and employment, which would improve the quality and longevity of their lives. This may take several generations.

To reject such assistance would mean their population would be a memory on the pages of history. Sir, there are more recommendations, however I deem these to be the most important."

Lord Carnarvon listened attentively, all the while stroking his lengthy white sideburns and mustache. With a grunt and cough he replied, "Major, you have spoken well and I believe have found issues that must be resolved. I will share your report and recommendations with the Colonial Secretary and have the House of Commons act on them expeditiously. Be sure to thank your wife Ellen for her support in this venture and the best of health to the both of you. Again, thank you."

His duties fulfilled, it was back home for Byron where his constituency work awaited him. Fortunately, he would be able to work from home. He had missed breakfast and tea with Ellen and trips to the nursery to check on their son. David was just approaching his first birthday when Ellen was expecting their second child. Would it be a girl this time? They would have to wait.

In due time Ellen gave birth to a baby girl with a trace of raven hair. Thankfully both mother and daughter were healthy. Byron could only stand by cradling David in his arms and admiring both mother and daughter. What should they name her? Neither Ellen nor Byron had known their mothers. They agreed to name their baby after both mothers. Ellen's mother was Margaret Victoria and Byron's mother, Kathryn Ann. After some thought they made the decision to use both of their mothers' names. Their first daughter would be named Kathryn Victoria, and if a second girl was born she would be named Margaret Ann. King Solomon could not have done any better.

The Fletcher family was a busy household, and it was about to get busier with the birth of a third child. Both parents were delighted it was a girl. As it was previously decided she was named Margaret Ann. After their third child, Ellen acquiesced and hired a nursemaid for the three children. Several additional servants helped make the Hamilton House run smoothly.

Byron was re-elected to serve West Dorset in parliament for the next twenty years until he retired from public office. During that time he continued to advise the minister of foreign affairs on the need for assistance in the education and health of New Zealand's Maori population. With three growing children he was interested in their education. At this time public education was available according to policy, but in reality was a disaster. Byron had some influence in establishing the Elementary Education Act of 1880, which required all children aged five to twelve attend primary school for a basic education. It was ineffective. Facilities were inadequate, teachers were unqualified, and attendance was erratic. Byron would not send his children to public schools.

DISCOVERY

Ben didn't understand what Eva meant when she said her name was Sarah. Confused, he uttered, "Eva what do you mean your name is Sarah?"

She was also confused, yet sure her name was Sarah.

"What should I call you, Eva or Sarah?"

"I don't know."

Ben continued, "Eva, for more than twenty-five years we have lived together and loved each other. We have three children we brought into this world. Thousands of miles have passed under us as we traveled all over England together. We only have each other and now I find out that you had another life, maybe with someone else." He felt uneasy about what she said. At this point in their lives would everything change? Had she been married? Did she have other children?

For the next several days their relationship was as chilly as the weather. After a week had passed they set the event aside and she accepted Ben calling her Eva.

A month later, Eva was having one of her restless nights and couldn't sleep, all the while thinking of the name Sarah. "Who was she? Why do I think about her? How can I find out who she is?" Eva got up, and looking out the old window saw a giant luminous pearl of a moon. She just stood staring at all its brightness. She closed her eyes and in a dream she saw herself walking down a road toward a river. She was frightened and felt she was about to fall in when the dream abruptly ended. As light from the moon cast shadows through her window, Eva returned to bed, pulled the blanked over her head and went to sleep.

When Ben woke up the next morning he could tell something had happened overnight. Eva seemed different. Curious, he asked, "Did you sleep well last night?"

"No. I had a scary dream."

"What was it?"

"I dreamt I was about to fall in a river, then the dream was suddenly over."

Ben did not know how to respond. Should he say anything? He remembered being with his father watching and hearing her fall in to the river. If he told her it was more than a dream, would it change their relationship? He responded with, "Well, you survived your dream." No more was said.

On a pleasant summer afternoon they decided to take a walk around the village when they were noticed by an older neighbor who invited them in for tea. They graciously accepted the invitation and the woman introduced herself as Adelle Beechworth. Ben responded by telling her they were Mr. & Mrs. Benjamin Warren, choosing not to use either Eva's or Sarah's name.

It was apparent that their hostess was the de facto matriarch of the village. Her grandfather had been the wealthy owner of the carpet factory and had left her with a generous inheritance. It enabled her to have the largest home in Thistleton. Eva noticed a beautiful spinning wheel next to a large fireplace. She asked whose it was and when Mrs. Beechworth confirmed that it was her own, asked Eva if she had ever used one. Without hesitation Eva responded, "Yes, my mother taught me how to spin wool when I was a young girl." Ben was astonished by what his wife said, and that she said it in such a casual manner. Their host so enjoyed their visit she invited them to stop by anytime.

On returning to their cottage Ben asked, "How did you remember your mother teaching you to spin when you were a young girl?"

Eva answered, "I don't know, I just remembered. It seemed normal to talk about it." Eva's memory did not come back like a dam bursting, rather like the trickle of water in a small meandering stream with multiple bends and curves. Her response to the spinning wheel was a start, a very slow start.

Ben knew what he had to do and that he should have done earlier, regardless of the consequences. He said, "Eva, I need to tell you something. My father was having our wagon repaired in the small village of Shillingstone, and while it was being fixed we camped on the bank of the River Stour. Later that night we were standing around a fire and saw you running into the river. You screamed and fell into the river and struck your head on a rock. My father and I rushed down and rescued you. I suppose that could have been when you lost your memory. You were with us for many days, then weeks, then years and never once did your memory return in all that time. It is only recently that I heard you say your name was Sarah." Eva's jaw dropped open and she stared blankly at Ben. It would take some time for her to understand what Ben had just told her.

In the meantime, Ben and Eva had financial concerns. Their savings would not last many years, and they needed additional income. They tried to sell their old caravan, but without success as there were fewer peddlers on England's roads, and the wagon was old and worn. Since it was parked just behind their home Ben decided to take it apart. After removing most of the top he was left with a box and four wheels like a farm wagon. Perhaps with some repairs and the purchase of an old horse it could be used as a wagon for hire. With Eva's agreement, Ben fixed the wagon and bought an old workhorse. Over a short period of time, he found work with his wagon which generated some income, but not enough for their needs.

He used the wagon to haul all kinds of items, including animal feed, stone, gravel, dirt, equipment, and furniture. One day he made a two mile trip to the village of South Witham to move furniture from a family estate. Among the items was an old spinning wheel which caught his attention. He wanted it for Eva, and in exchange he agreed to move the family's items at no cost. Eva was surprised and pleased when Ben arrived home with a spinning wheel. Their cottage was small, but they would make a place for such a wonderful addition.

Both had an activity they found rewarding, Ben's wagon service created income, and Sarah found spinning wool somehow soothing. She never considered that it might improve her lost memory.

Some skills are never lost and even after so many years without a spinning wheel she still remembered how to spin wool. Ben brought home some clean lamb's wool and two carding paddles needed for preparing the wool for spinning. Soon spinning wool was as easy as eating or sleeping and it gave her time to think. Could the spinning wheel open the door to her memory? She remembered the mother who taught her to spin. But what was her mother like, and what of her father? Was there someone she loved before she lost her memory? Did she have a family? Eva felt her memory was locked tight and she had yet to find a key.

Over the next year she had several remembrances about her past life, and they always came while she was spinning. One afternoon Eva remembered a father who had loved her, but that love had come with obligations. What were they? Months later she recalled a Maypole festival and the joy of being with someone special, but who? The festival was similar to many she had seen in her travels around the country.

Later in the year Eva was sitting on her stool spinning wool when her mind suddenly came alive with the memory of a young man who was her greatest joy and greatest sorrow. Who was he? The thought of him was troubling. At times she wished these thoughts would stop streaming through her mind, but they kept coming. A word that kept coming back to her was Shillingstone. When she had asked Ben, he had told her it was a small village, but little else.

The moment he walked in the front door, Eva asked, "Ben, tell me more about Shillingstone. I don't remember anything about it."

Ben answered, "It was near Shillingstone that you had your accident. Ten years later we spent two days there to have our wagon repaired. During that time you and the children stayed at the Old Ox Inn for two days. You walked around the village, visited some people in their home, but you didn't recognize anyone, nor did anyone recognized you. I didn't know that it could have been your home."

Eva thought about what he said and replied, "Things come back only in bits and pieces. I can't put anything together. My mind is like a dark cloudy day with the sun poking through a few holes in the clouds. Ben, you used the word home. Shillingstone was likely my home and my life prior the accident. I have to go there and discover my past."

Ben was silent for a few moments and then told her, "Eva, we can't. We have enough to live on now with a small amount saved for the future. It would likely take all we have with no assurance that it would help. I'm so very sorry, but you know what I'm saying is true."

She didn't want to agree, but she did. Eva would never find out about the life she had lived in her village. An exciting prospect to discover her lost life was dashed. She knew where it could be found, but was unable to go and find it.

The pleasant Eva that Ben had known was now morose and sullen. Her life as Sarah disappeared in the river, and was being lost again. There was more to be found than just the snippets of her memory that had recently been uncovered. She had many sleepless nights going over and over again what little information had come back to her. Eva could not put the pieces together and she was coming to believe it would have been better to have known nothing than to know so little. She withdrew from Ben and everyone else while her spinning wheel sat in the corner gathering dust. In her deepest distress she remembered searing words she had heard somewhere before: *Hope is lost... hope is lost.*

Ben was confused and frustrated, as he had never experienced Eva acting so miserably. Who was he living with, Eva or Sarah? He knew Eva, but knew nothing about Sarah. Their life together would likely fall apart if this continued. While thinking about this at the kitchen table, he looked at her spinning wheel sitting idle in a corner of their living room. Until recently she had enjoyed using it. He started a fire in the hearth and tried to think of ideas to help Eva.

All his life he had been buying and selling products, but could he do it again? It would be impossible to market inferior goods and have repeat buyers while remaining in one location. What could he make or produce? Nothing. Once more Ben glanced at Eva's unused spinning wheel and found his answer. With his help she could spin wool, and he could sell it using his wagon to reach area market towns. Ben was excited about the possibilities. He would sell the idea to Eva that it would be possible to raise enough money to travel to Shillingstone.

He made a fresh pot of tea, and asked Eva to sit with him at their kitchen table. Ben, the salesman, was about to make an important pitch. It was all about selling Shillingstone. He explained his plan and how they could make enough money for Eva to discover her life where it had been lost. He suggested that they might earn enough money to also visit their children. Eva was quiet and deep in thought. Ben had been faithful and had always been a hard worker. She appreciated what he wanted to do for her. Finally she smiled, reached over to Ben and gave him a kiss. Perchance she would find the life she had lost.

CHILDREN

Children of wealthy families had the option of attending private schools or to being tutored at home. Byron and Ellen chose to hire tutors for David, Kathryn and Margaret. When they were five, they began to read and write. In the following years they were taught mathematics, science, history, grammar, French and classic literature.

In 1885 David turned 13 and his parents decided to enroll him in the Sherborne boarding school for boy's ages13 through 18. Its six-year curriculum was designed to prepare young men for a university education. At Sherborne David would live in one of five houses and come home for holidays and summer months. Ellen and Byron also appreciated that the Sherborne campus was only sixteen miles west of their home.

It was a different story for Kathryn and Margaret. No one was more aware of their educational challenges than their mother. Higher education was essentially not available. Instead, young girls were encouraged to attend private finishing schools. The objective of such schools was for girls to be prepared for marriage and to have children. Ellen had been down that path and did not want it for her daughters. While David was at Sherborne, Ellen continued having tutors for her girls' education, including some refinement and graces that they would have learned at a finishing school.

Over the years as a Member of Parliament, Byron had maintained an office in General Hamilton's town house in London. He became aware of a school in London for young ladies called Bedford College. On a trip to London, Ellen joined him for a visit to the campus. After a tour of the magnificent founder's building and an interview with the staff they decided this was the place for their girls.

After David graduated from Sherborne he enrolled at St. Georges University Medical School. He had decided to practice medicine on the North Island of New Zealand. His father had been a soldier/administrator on this island and he wanted to walk in those footsteps, however as a medical doctor to the Maori rather than a soldier.

Kathryn finished her degree in science from Bedford College in 1900. While in London she met a young lawyer and became engaged to be married. Byron and Ellen approved of her decision.

Two years later Margaret completed a degree in linguistics and planned to continue her education for a doctorate in Egyptology.

It is unlikely that Byron had ever spent much time musing about his life, past, present or future. Perhaps it was an auspicious time to do so now that he was 65 and about to face a new century in 1900. Fifty years ago he was just a young farm boy who in several years would fall in love, would have his marriage proposal delayed for years, and would make an impetuous decision to leave home. In retrospect it was that choice which started him on a path he never could have imagined and would continue through to his 65th year.

He had given no serious thought to where he would go or what he would do. His first step on that path had been a happenstance meeting with a crusty old retired Sergeant at the Old Ox Inn and the beginning of a lifelong friendship. Sergeant Wilson directed him to a military career that would eventually cover nearly a third of his life. During those years more had happened than he ever thought possible.

Byron had served in three different military regiments in the British army and had risen from a naive private to the rank of Major. He had participated in battles in three different countries and had been rewarded by receiving England's highest honor, the Victoria Cross. The most important event that came out of those years was meeting a beautiful young woman who had become the love of his life, Lady Ellen.

He felt the most noteworthy part of this life was not his 14 years serving his country in the military, it was the following quarter century that he served his country as a Member of Parliament. Byron played a part in numerous bills passed by the parliament that had improved the lives of his constituency and that of greater England. Ellen was one of the motivating factors in his political career during those years and she had been just as important as a mother and educator of their three children. Byron believed they were blessed with exceptional children in David, Kathryn and Margaret. New Zealand had been a large part of Byron's military and political life and he was pleased that David would follow in his footsteps and serve as a medical doctor in the North Island

His father Howard had been proud of Byron's accomplishments, but toward the end of his life he still harbored an unfulfilled wish that his son become the fourth generation to work the family farm. Unknown to him, it had become Byron's wish as well. Crops had not been planted on the farm for decades and Byron decided to change that by getting dirt under his fingernails for the first time in many years. He decided to become a gentleman farmer and fulfill his father's hopes, which would be realized. Byron wished to be remembered for his distinctive military career, for being a noteworthy Member of Parliament, and for being a thriving farmer.

Both Byron and Ellen were grateful for their lives in Hamilton House, their wonderful children, and for being able to well in the village of Shillingstone. They hoped and prayed that God would continue to bless their lives for a long time.

WARREN'S WOOL

Ben decided to act on the invitation that Mrs. Beechworth had extended during their last visit. When they arrived, she was pleased to see them again. Mrs. Beechworth was an observant individual and thought it likely that her guests were living with meager financial resources. It had been some time since she had helped someone, and she believed it was time to do so now.

After they were seated, Mrs. Beechworth said, "It has been a long time since there has been any excitement or energy in Thistleton, and that needs to change. I believe that both of you can be the instruments of that change. Eva, I have seen some of the wool you have spun and they are some very fine skeins. Ben, you are in good health and have energy and experience in purchasing products. It would be up to you to procure wool from local sheep farmers and then, wash, dry and card the wool to get it ready for spinning. Sarah can do the spinning. There are many villages in the area that would be delighted to purchase some of the very finest skeins of wool." After letting this sink in she added, "There are two benefits from such a venture. First, you will derive some financial benefit, perhaps more than you think. Second, our lethargic village will come alive with the reputation of having some of the best quality wool in Rutland. This is a lot to think about and details need to be addressed, but it can be successful."

Mrs. Beechworth suggested that they look at this venture as a family business. It would start modestly, and develop as sales increased. At first she would supply the financing, Ben would gather the material, and Sarah would generate the product. Each would have one third ownership with a plan that it would eventually be owned by Ben and Eva. Mrs. Beechworth suggested that they take a couple of days to think about it and then they would talk again.

Ben and Sarah looked at each other and were astonished by her offer. It was almost the exact plan that Ben had told to Sarah, nearly word for word. There was nothing in her offer they had to think about. Ben responded, "Mrs. Beechworth, thank you for your generous offer. It was quite unexpected. We will take your advice and review your plan and visit again in several days." With appreciation they left and returned home.

Ben was sure the entire village had heard Eva's scream of excitement. How did Mrs. Beechworth know what they were planning to do? He only intended to ask her for ideas and recommendations on how to put his plan into reality. Both were thankful that they didn't have to explain the real reason they needed the money.

Early in the morning of day two Ben and Eva were at Mrs. Beechworth's door and eager to hear more of her plans. She was pleased to see them. Before talking about what she had in mind Mrs. Beechworth wanted them to know more about herself. While her grandfather owned the carpet factory, she had managed the business for 25 years before it was sold. At the time of the sale it was a thriving company, but the buyer mismanaged the business and had to file for bankruptcy. It had been ten years since the factory had closed.

At first Mrs. Beechworth managed everything, with Eva the producer, and Ben sourcing the material needed. She knew who had raw wool to sell, and it was up to Ben to collect it, wash it, dry it and card it and for Eva to spin into finished skeins of wool. A skein or ball of finished wool weighed about an ounce. Eva estimated that she could spin up to one pound of wool a day. Mrs. Beechworth knew of individuals and shops who were buyers of finely spun wool. They were in business with all partners doing their best to make it a success.

In the first month their venture made a small profit, pleasing all three owners. But Eva was wearing out from the pressure of work. Her hands were sore and her arms and back ached from hours at her spinning wheel. She needed help. Two local spinners were hired who could work in their own homes.

After seven months they had a very profitable business. Eva was drained yet excited that she and Ben had enough money to travel to Shillingstone. They did well enough to add a visit to Shrewsbury to visit Ruth. Mrs. Beechworth only needed to know that they were going to visit their family.

Before leaving home they agreed to use Eva as her name when in Shillingstone. They had exchanged telegrams with Sophia and set the day they hoped to arrive. She invited Ben and Sarah to stay with her, but they chose to stay at an inn.

The railway station closest to Thistleton was eight miles distant from the village of Oakham. From Oakham station they planned take a train to London and then on to Shrewsbury. Sophia telegraphed that she had arranged their transportation from the station to the inn and then to her home. She was as pleased to see Ben and Eva as they were to see her. After greeting her mother and father, Ruth told them that she and Stephen were in love and planned to be married within the year. Ruth also told her mother that she had no knowledge of either Lilly or Thomas. There was little alternative but to accept the reality that they would likely never see them again.

After an enjoyable dinner and a short visit with Sophia, Ben and Eva retired to their inn. They were exhausted but pleased they had come. Lying in bed Eva asked Ben if he had seen some strange metal objects in the house. What were they? Ben had noticed them as well and told her they were likely some old surveyor's tools. All Eva could say was, "Oh."

SHILLINGSTONE

The following morning Ben and Eva said their goodbyes to Ruth, Stephen, and Sophia. They then boarded the train for Shillingstone. With a distance of 185 miles it would take the better part of the day, including stops and starts. Eva had no ideas or plans for what they would do when they arrived. In just hours she and Ben would step from the train and their feet would be planted on the platform in the village where her life had begun. No one would greet her, recognize her or know her.

It was a pleasant late summer day with a blue sky and shining sun as passengers stepped down on the station platform. Some were greeted by friends and family, while others scurried to collect their belongings from the baggage car and proceed to one of the waiting carriages. In less than thirty minutes all who were on the platform were gone except for Ben and Eva, and the train was a long distance down the tracks. To make his wife feel more comfortable, Ben reminded Eva that they had been here fifteen years ago to have their wagon repaired. Eva vaguely remembered her two days at an inn, and caring for their children before leaving early in the morning. In spite of that she felt like she was in an unfamiliar village.

Ben asked the stationmaster for directions to the inn. He told them it was about a mile and a half down Blandford Road. They could walk or he would try to arrange for a pony and trap for them. With only a small valise, they decided to walk. Halfway to the inn they reached the village center. For

Eva it seemed no different than hundreds of places she and Ben had visited. Ben felt the same until he came upon the blacksmith's forge. He remembered having been there twice for repairs on the wagon, but he didn't recognize the smithy who paid no attention to an old couple who had stopped to watch him work.

By the time they got to the Old Ox Inn it was well into evening. Eva remembered the inn and how difficult it was to handle three small children for two days in a room not much bigger than their wagon. After they took a room and freshened up they came down for an evening meal. It had been a long tiring day and they decided to turn in for the night. Ben went to sleep quickly, but not Eva. Lying in bed, she felt emotionally drained. She had hoped that just being in Shillingstone would give her a feeling of having come home, but no such impression came. She was hoping to find something, a place, a person, a shop, anything she could remember, but her mind was empty. Perhaps tomorrow she would remember something from her past life.

Ben woke up before Eva and began to think about the day ahead. The memory of his previous visit was intact in his mind, but his life was not divided into two parts like Eva's. He wasn't looking for anything for himself. It was all about Eva. Ben had some concerns about what she might discover from her past life and how that might disrupt their lives.

At breakfast Eva asked Ben if he had any thoughts about how they should proceed. He told her he had asked the innkeeper to make arrangements for a horse and trap from the livery and by midmorning they were on the road. A logical starting point was where Eva's accident had occurred. They went down Blandford Road past the railway station toward the river. Ben was not sure he could find the exact spot where Eva had walked and had fallen in the river, however it was not far from the village. They stopped and walked down to the river's edge, but it triggered no response in her mind.

From there they returned and wound their way around the village roads to see if Eva recognized any places. She didn't. Ben saw a church and decided to check it out. He went past a home called Church House, parked the trap and walked through the cemetery to the Church of the Holy Rood. It was open and they entered and sat in one of the pews. It was likely the first time in over 25 years that they had been in a church. Church attendance had never been a part of their lives. Eva commented on the beauty of the church, but had no emotional response.

From the church they rode down Church Road, noticing that most of the houses were large and well kept, including one called Hamilton House. Soon they were back at the Old Ox Inn. Between waiting for the horse trap and their travels through town, the day was coming to an end and the evening meal was about to be served.

Sitting at their table they evaluated the day. What had they discovered, other than Shillingstone was a pleasant village? Nothing. Ben was relieved, but Eva was frustrated. They had spent all this time, money and energy and knew no more than when they had left Thistleton. As they prepared for the night they passed the innkeeper and for some unknown reason Eva blurted out, "We came all the way here, to get some information on a lost woman and found nothing!"

He heard what she said and asked, "A lost woman you say. How long ago?"

She replied, "Possibly 25 years or more."

The innkeeper pointed to an old man with a full white beard, perhaps 90 or more years of age, sitting in a corner holding an empty glass. He told Eva, "That bloke's retired military, been around here for years, knows or knew most people in these parts. You bring him a fresh pint of beer, and he'll warm right up to you. But let me warn you, once you get him talking he don't quit. You might need to walk away and leave him mumbling."

Ben spoke up. "I'll take him a pint."

They approached the old man and asked, "Will you have a pint, and do you mind if we join you?"

The old man squinted with eyes half closed and then spoke, "Yes indeed, sit down, sit down, I'm by myself and I like company. Name's Wilson, folks 'round here call me Sarge."

Eva took over from Ben and commented, "We're visitors here and have heard a story of a woman who disappeared years ago, but no one seems to remember what happened."

Wilson was quiet for a while as he was conjuring up the past and thinking. Then he replied, "You mean Sarah?"

Eva was about to say yes, but stopped. All she could think of was to say, "No one mentioned a name."

Up to now Wilson had been casual and relaxed but started to become animated. He declared, "She was a damn good woman. Had an aunt, Edith, who was my wife, God bless her soul. She died three years ago. Sarah never married, was supposed to, but waited too long and he married someone else. No one knows what happened, she…she just disappeared."

Eva really wanted to know everything, but didn't want the sergeant to feel interrogated. She wanted to know about Sarah's family and asked, "I suppose she had family?"

He responded in gruff tones, "Dammed good family, didn't deserve such tragedy. Her brother died young, and mother, not sure why, died some years later. Damn bloody father left his daughter alone for a widow, I think in Shrewsbury, and the bastard died a year or two later."

"You asked if she got married. My wife was upset that Sarah turned down a good man. When he married someone else, Edith said she fell apart."

Eva was anxious to know who the good man was, but didn't want to appear overly interested, and casually mentioned, "I suppose he was from around here?"

At this point Wilson was excited to tell her, "Byron Fletcher! By God he was and still is, a good and courageous man. He arose to the rank of major in the army, became a member of parliament, and married a general's daughter. He and his wife have three marvelous children. They live on Church Street, a short distance from here. He stops to visit here now and again and we talk for hours about the wars..."

Eva did have one more thought and said, "I'm curious, if over all those years she was missing, did anyone recognize any woman who might look like her?"

Wilson did not reply, but stroked his scraggy white beard, and looked stumped by the question. Finally he spoke, "Let's see, years back a travelling family passed through here and several people thought the wife might look a little like Sarah. They moved on before folks would know. Nothing since then."

Eva rose from her chair as she had heard enough. And the innkeeper was right, the sergeant would talk all night. She told him, "We must get up early and be on our way in the morning. Your story has been very interesting. Ben and I thank you for sharing it with us."

"Sure you don't want to hear more? Wilson began to mumble and carried on although he no longer had an audience.

In their room, Eva could not sleep. She felt strange that Wilson had been talking about her and didn't know it. When she heard the name Byron she felt a shiver through her body which she could not explain.

Ben had listened intently, trying to navigate through the Sargent's story. He didn't believe Sarah's life had been very happy.

Ben and Eva left the next morning and arrived back in Thistleton late in the afternoon. It felt good to be home. They were too tired to think any more about their journey and would talk about it in the morning.

Their first order of business after breakfast was to check in with Mrs. Beechworth. She was pleased to see them and assured them that she was kept busy overseeing production and sales. Every day it reminded her of directing her grandfather's business.

When they saw how much work had to be done, Ben and Eva changed their plans to work most of the day and then chat about their trip after supper. Ben had recently purchased a lovely pair of Windsor chairs with curved arms, and they enjoyed the comfort, sitting in front of the fireplace.

After moments of silence Eva shared some of the thoughts that had been bouncing around in her head most of the day: "Ben, thank you for your help and understanding during this entire trip. I did remember two days in Shillingstone when our wagon was repaired. Most of my effort then was taking care of three active little children. Nothing we saw while riding around the village stirred my memory. Sergeant Wilson was helpful with some details about my family. Apparently, every family member has died, my brother, my mother, my father and my aunt Edith. The only living person who would have any interest in knowing I am alive is the one I was to marry, Byron. I remember nothing about him."

Ben had listened intently and finally said, "After more than 25 years of struggling to make a living and raising three children, we are experiencing the best years of our lives. We have a home without wheels, sufficient money to live on and we are a part of the life of our village. I have always been called Ben because that is who I am. You have always been called Eva and that is how I have always known you. Now, who are you Eva or Sarah? I know one, but not the other."

Eva was speechless! She had never thought of it in those terms. Almost everyone she knew prior to her disappearance was dead, and she had been long dead to everyone who knew her. The only person who might want to know that she was still alive was Byron. She thought contacting him would not change his life in any way, but at least he would know that the Sarah he knew was alive. Deep in the core of her existence she wanted him to know she was not dead.

She finally responded to Ben, "We have a good life and have each other, for which I am pleased. In time I will have this sorted out." With that, Ben was satisfied that all was well and went off to bed.

Eva remained by the fireplace thinking about all that had happened in Shillingstone. The only person with knowledge about her life as Sarah was Byron. She thought if she could only speak to him and ask a question about Sarah it might resolve the gnawing question of who she was. She decided to write a letter to Byron and ask if he would be willing to fill in the blanks in her memory. There would be no harm in doing that and it would benefit her greatly. With pen and paper she started her letter:

Major Fletcher: I am certain this will come as a shock to you. I am Sarah Glanville and I am not dead. Years ago I fell in the Stour River, struck my head, and lost my memory for many years. Only recently has it begun to come back. You are the only living person who can tell me about my life as Sarah. Presently I have two lives, one as Sarah and another as Eva all these years after my accident. I need your help to find out who I am: I am writing to know if you would be willing to help me?
Yours respectfully, Sarah.

Eva folded the letter and put it in the pocket of her smock, intending to mail it the next day. She joined Ben in bed, but sleep did not come quickly.

The following day Ben was off collecting wool from local farmers, and Eva was spinning on her wheel. Numerous times she reached into her pocket to be sure the letter was still there. Uncertain about what she should do, she decided to wait another day to mail her letter. It had been a busy two days and she looked forward to the comfort of their home and an evening with Ben. To Eva's disappointment Ben was tired when he returned and told her he was off to bed.

Still wearing her smock Eva took the letter out of her pocket and carefully read it one more time. Then she folded it over, sealed it, laid it on the table and planned to mail it in the morning. She felt nervously excited thinking about Byron receiving it. She would finally be able to discover her past life. All she had to do was mail that letter. She had no recollection of how long she sat near the warmth of the fireplace, staring at the letter on the table. It would solve all questions of her identity, or would it? Eva got up, gathered the letter in her hand and started for the bedroom. After a few steps she stopped, paused for a moment, then slowly walked back to the fireplace and carefully placed the letter on the glowing embers. In seconds it was gone.

ACKNOWLEDGEMENTS

My friend Doug Greener has been an invaluable mentor in writing this novel. His guidance, recommendations and encouragement has been greatly appreciated. In addition three individuals, Mary Holms, Claire Parr and Marilyn Goodman were very helpful in grammar review and proof reading the manuscript.

Numerous others read early versions of the manuscript and were helpful with suggestions and encouragement about the story. My daughter Elizabeth and husband Troy volunteered Antares, their IT service, to aid in the self-printing process. Robert Deichert was the point person who accomplish this technical task.

Nathan Clark, owner of Immure Records, designed the creative exterior covers of the book.

ABOUT THE AUTHOR

Keith McConnell was born in Toronto, Ontario, Canada in 1939, however most his life was spent in Winnipeg, Manitoba.

In 1959 he moved to St. Paul, Minnesota to attend Bethel College and Seminary. There he received a BA degree in 1963 and a Master of Divinity degree in 1966.

For a short time he served ministerial duties, then moved on to spend the remainder of his career in every aspect of Real Estate, retiring in 2008.

Now retired, Keith and Carol make their home in New Brighton, Minnesota. Over the years he received the moniker of a "story teller" which eventually led to writing many of them down. This, his first novel, was one of them. It eventually developed into the current historical/fiction novel.

Visit: www.KeithMcConnell.com

Printed in Great Britain
by Amazon

57687973R00163